IN HIS HANDS

Sophie Berecz and Arpad Soo

Pacific Press® Publishing Association
Nampa, Idaho
Oshawa, Ontario, Canada
www.pacificpress.com

Edited by Tim Lale
Cover photo by The Special Photographers Co./PHOTONICA
Cover design by Dennis Ferree
Inside design by Steve Lanto

Copyright © 2002 by
Pacific Press® Publishing Association
Printed in the United States of America

Scripture taken from THE HOLY BIBLE, New International Version, copyright © 1973, 1978, 1984 International Bible Society. Used by permission of Zondervan Bible Publishers.

Additional copies of this book may be purchased at
http://www.adventistbookcenter.com

ISBN 0-8163-1903-0

02 03 04 05 • 5 4 3 2 1

This book is dedicated to God,
Who risked first, giving all for us.

Arpad
Also to my parents, Karoly and Rozalia, who started me
on my journey;
to my wife, Adela, who sustains me in my journey;
and to my three sons, Arpad, Norbert, and Zoltan, who
motivate me
to continue my journey.

Sophie
To Monty

Contents

CHAPTER 1.	Dead End	7
CHAPTER 2.	The Interrogation	14
CHAPTER 3.	A Matter of Time	21
CHAPTER 4.	The Furnace	32
CHAPTER 5.	Waiting	38
CHAPTER 6.	The Strategy	43
CHAPTER 7.	Black Market	49
CHAPTER 8.	Hungry People	54
CHAPTER 9.	The Message	59
CHAPTER 10.	The Double Compartment	66
CHAPTER 11.	Plan C	72
CHAPTER 12.	Darkness	75
CHAPTER 13.	The Sign	78
CHAPTER 14.	A New Twist	82
CHAPTER 15.	Half of Heaven	89
CHAPTER 16.	Paradise Lost	94
CHAPTER 17.	The Journey North	99
CHAPTER 18.	Resurrection	107
CHAPTER 19.	Up the Ladder	112
CHAPTER 20.	Something More	119
CHAPTER 21.	Lost and Found	126
CHAPTER 22.	Heaven's Floodgates	132
CHAPTER 23.	A Good Measure	140
CHAPTER 24.	Stronghold	146
CHAPTER 25.	The Bold Question	151
CHAPTER 26.	Another Gate	157

Dead End

For the fifth day, Arpad Soo[*] paced his cage. Never in his twenty-nine years had he felt this useless, this trapped. The unspoken verdict burned into his mind. *They will take me back to Romania. That's five to twenty-five years for smuggling and another twenty-five for escaping. No!*

The words of his wife, Ildiko, echoed in his mind. "Are you sure this will work?" she had asked, looking anxious before she boarded the airport bus. She had not wanted the fake Yugoslavian visa in the first place.

"Of course. Don't worry," Arpad had soothed. "I'll pick you up in Belgrade in a few hours, then we'll find a way into Austria." Ildiko's face had questioned him. "We will!" he had insisted. "Everything will be fine." He would meet up with his wife in Yugoslavia and smuggle her over the border into Austria, request political asylum, then send for the boys. For the first time in their lives, they would be free. Why shouldn't he be confident? God had never let him down.

---

[*] Pronounced Arpod Show.

Not until now, it seemed. Arpad was now under arrest in a foreign land, his wife imprisoned in another, and both his family and church members were abandoned as he faced becoming a prisoner for life.

Prisoners of the Communists, particularly smugglers, are not treated like welcome houseguests, unless a breakfast of brittle toast and lukewarm tea count. His stomach growled.

In the Czechoslovakian prison cell that measured twelve by eight feet, the walls sweated like a damp cellar. A bed made of a few splintered planks stood along the farthest cement wall with a thin gray blanket and dank pillow rumpled on top. A stinking squat hole in the corner and a pushbutton for water were the only facilities. Daylight fell through a barred window, small and out of reach above his head. Arpad studied the striped pattern for a while, his forehead crinkled with worry. *Where is God when I need Him?*

Rubbing his hands over the stubble on his chin and his rough mustache, he covered his face, trying to shut out the mental pictures that wouldn't stop coming. He sat slouched on the bed and listened to the far-off grate of a cell door as it opened and closed then the tramp of heavy boots fading away. Though it was 1984, the jail seemed disconnected from time, like a clock with frozen hands. He watched a black spider crawl toward the window. Arpad stood, restless, his legs aching from inactivity, and began to tread the well-worn floor.

Why is this happening? He stared out of the cell bars of the door at the peeling paint outside his cell. *Is this what God has in mind?* The events of his capture replayed through his thoughts. *Romania. Prison. Fifty years?* His mind grappled with the concept. Then the faces of his two little boys shot through his memory. Thank God they were safe with his wife's parents.

Ildiko's anxious face tormented him. *"Everything will be fine."* The words mocked him. They were a steady throb, a scraping of nails over slate, a nausea. *I was so close to freedom. How could I have been so irresponsible? Not only have I ruined*

Dead End

my life, but the lives of my family and my church members. I was trying to serve You, God. How could You lead me through such powerful ways, only to have me at a dead end here? Where did You go?

There was little hope now that he was caught, but this fact still didn't seem real to Arpad. Maybe the Lord would have mercy. It was a thin belief, frayed with knowledge of what always happened in Communist countries. He remembered the Bible story of the apostle Peter who was miraculously set free by an angel while the guards slept. It left Arpad with a hollow pit in his stomach. No angel had ever freed the Peters in his life.

Though the Czechoslovakian authorities had threatened and interrogated him daily, Arpad had only told the truth. Daily for eight years, he had risked his life smuggling truth, precious literature for the spiritually starving Romanian churches, time and again escaping capture. How ironic that he should be caught now, when he wasn't smuggling anything.

"God, I'm not ready for this," Arpad pleaded. "My family needs me. My churches need me." Communist authorities didn't favor pastors, especially pastors who disobeyed the law. When the Czechs returned him to the Romanian authorities, he would be finished, imprisoned for life in terrible conditions. Had he done all he could for God? Was his use over? Was this how it was going to be? *Gone,* he agonized. *My life is gone.*

More pictures flickered across his mind, but this time he didn't fight them. They were all he had. *God, You were there when I was a child. I had faith in You.* He slumped on the bed again, remembering. The walls in this new memory were white, and a draw-curtain hanging from the ceiling separated him from the other patients in beds with metal railings. He was still a prisoner.

* * *

"My Lord, the One who loves me, will heal me," sang three-year-old Arpad from the hospital bed in which he lay, completely paralyzed. His wide eyes looked up at his mother sitting on a stool beside the bed, her head covered by a dark shawl, her hands holding his, and her voice soothing him, keeping him brave. The white curtain ruffled as a nurse and a doctor stepped into the small partition.

"Singing again?" the doctor said with a chuckle. "How's our little preacher doing?" He felt Arpad's forehead. Arpad's forehead was burning, though to him his whole body felt frozen. He tried to move his neck, but his body wasn't listening. The song he had learned from his mother began again, though softer. "My Lord, the One who loves me, will heal me," Arpad repeated.

The doctor shook his head. "He's so confident," he whispered, turning to Arpad's mother. "Unfortunately, no one with this dramatic a case of polio will recover without severe damage." His mother winced, looking at her tiny son, but Arpad only blinked at the ceiling.

"My Lord, the One who loves me, will heal me," his small voice continued. The doctor smiled sadly and left.

From his earliest memory, people called Arpad the Little Preacher because he often shared his faith by raising his voice in songs of praise. Arpad was unashamed of his God in Communist Romania, where believing in God was an embarrassment for the majority. His father, a Seventh-day Adventist pastor who cared for five little churches in the Romanian villages, worked hard to support the family of six.

Always traveling from town to town, Pastor Soo tried to teach the villagers God's message despite a complete lack of lesson materials or songbooks for worship. After 1949 the government had allowed no religious publications to be circulated or printed in Romania. Consequently, the few remaining devotional books, songbooks, and Bibles were falling apart. Because Arpad's father knew how to do bookbinding, he picked up the tattered books from his district churches, brought them home, and then glued, patched, bound, and covered them, taking them back to their owners four weeks later. His church members paid him a small fee for doing these services. Then when his sons were old enough, he put them to work too, paying them a portion of the money.

From the fifth grade on, Arpad learned to be self-supporting. His father made only a minimum-wage salary from the financially struggling churches. It was possible to support his family only because of his bookbinding, supplemented with food donations from his church members. Because the Romanian government forced most of the villagers to be farmers, many of his church members, like the Israelites in the Old Testament, brought their first crops to the church for the support of their beloved pastor.

Green and brown fields checkered the rolling hills and valleys through northern Transylvania, where Arpad's family lived. Dusty blue skies washed across isolated farms, contrasting with the white grazing sheep, before thinning into the high Carpathian mountain range. Fifteen miles away from these peaks, the village of St. George proceeded at a slower pace than the growing industrial cities of the nation. In the central plaza, children played in the fountains, and old men dozed on benches. Before World War II, this land belonged to Hungary, but in that war the boundary line was moved and Romania took over, making the Hungarians aliens in their own country.

The Soos were as Hungarian as the little town in which they lived. They ate soup with every meal, along with fresh chopped onions, sour cream, and bread. Arpad, Istvan, Marta, and Gabriella lived with their parents in a tiny two-story apartment looking across a narrow street at identical apartments. Their family was among the poorest of the poor, so Arpad's mother became an expert at sewing patches on clothes. She wove the stitches so well that the squares blocking the holes didn't show. The family wore the same clothes to church on Sabbath as they did the rest of the week, washing and pressing them on Friday. When Arpad and his brother and sisters outgrew their shoes, his mother cut the nose out of the shoes so they could wear them longer. When the heels wore down, they were taken to the shoemaker and patched. The Soo family discarded nothing.

Living the Christian faith in Romania during the 1950s proved difficult. The government clenched its fist around nearly every factory, farm, shop, and church in the country, holding a tight grasp over religion especially. Though the government opposed religion, in order to keep popular support it tolerated public worship by fourteen religions, Seventh-day Adventism being one of the lucky few.

In this difficult environment the Soo family taught their children dependence on God for everything—even when the dreaded polio struck. At the time there was no vaccine for this widespread disease that crippled, maimed, and paralyzed thousands of children throughout Europe in the 1950s. Arpad had one of the worst cases. For treatment he was dipped twice a day into hot wax. As the thick wax enclosed around him, Arpad could feel the burning heat. Every morning and evening he suffered in the hot liquid for twenty to thirty minutes. "My Lord, the One who loves me, will heal me," he sang. Arpad never gave up.

At a union-wide meeting of all the Adventist pastors, the attendees continually brought little Arpad's condition before the Lord. Of all childhood polio victims, the doctors told them, 99 percent were left with some debilitation, an arm or leg that wouldn't grow or that remained crippled. Needing a brace, crutch, or wheelchair was not uncommon.

Of the 276 cases of polio that year, only Arpad healed completely. The doctors and nurses were shocked, but it didn't seem a surprise to Arpad. Six weeks after leaving the hospital he had total movement of his body. Three months later the Little Preacher was running.

Four years later, he was still running, sliding across the fresh, shining wax on his mother's hardwood floor. His

Dead End

family lived on the second floor of the German-style apartment complex, the rooms barely large enough for four growing children. The lower apartment served as the church where Arpad's father preached. In the middle of the complex was an inside courtyard blocked off from the street by two iron gates, ten feet wide and fourteen feet tall, connecting two apartment buildings. In between the gate and the courtyard ran an arching tunnel forty feet long, the tunnel floor gently sloping from the higher courtyard down to the busy street outside. The street in front served as a major thoroughfare for town traffic headed to the railroad station.

The inside courtyard was a perfect playground for the kids. One afternoon, Arpad, his brother and sisters, and his neighborhood friends were playing "cat and mouse," a favorite game.

"Tag, you're it."

"You better run," called his older brother, turning for his first victim to seven-year-old Arpad. "I'm going to catch you."

"No you can't!" Arpad yelled. He glanced around the stony courtyard where his friends were running, his brother closing in on him. Through the long tunnel to the street, he saw the gate slightly opened. *I'll run down the tunnel, duck outside the gate, and around the corner,* Arpad schemed. *He'll catch me if I turn back.* Arpad dashed down the sloping tunnel, gaining momentum. He pushed through the gate, and flew onto the short sidewalk. Trying to turn, his foot caught on a crack in the sidewalk. Stumbling, his body hurtled him out into the middle of the street.

Too far. Too late.

His mother, shaking a rug out from their apartment balcony above the tunnel, saw the ten-wheeler dump truck plow toward her son. It hit him with its metal bumper, knocking him flat on the pavement, and rolling over him. She didn't have time to scream.

The Interrogation

"Arpad!" his mother shrieked, almost leaping from the balcony. Passersby ran to the small body lying sprawled in the middle of the street. The children stopped short, breathlessly emerging from the tunnel behind him. His sister screamed. The dump truck screeched to a stop forty feet past the boy. The driver jumped out, his face contorted and green with horror. A crowd began to gather.

Arpad had felt a blow, heard the screams, and saw strangers running toward him. Scared by the excitement, he lay still. *What just happened?* he wondered. Strong arms lifted him from the pavement. His mother, weeping, ran out of the front door, almost throwing herself on him.

"I'm OK. I'm OK." Arpad wiggled out of the stranger's arms, brushing himself off. His mother reached for him, searching from head to toe for injuries, crying and scolding Arpad all the while.

"I'm really OK," he reassured her. The crowd stared, unbelieving. "Did you see the size of that truck?" a voice murmured. "Did you see how fast it hit him?" another echoed.

There wasn't a scratch.

The Interrogation

* * *

In the jail cell, Arpad stared at his hands. *You obviously had something in mind for these, God*, he mused. *You saved me for a special work, but are You finished with me now?*

Bang. The lock rattled, and the iron door scraped open. A Czech guard in khaki uniform stepped in, an almost welcome relief.

"Come," the guard grunted in the Czech language while motioning Arpad out of the cell.

"It's the examining room today, is it?" Arpad replied. "At least I can get out of my cell." The guard couldn't understand Arpad's Romanian, but he whacked Arpad hard on the legs with his heavy club. Arpad counted the steps to where he was going, where he had gone twice a day, every day, for the past four miserable days, where, it seemed, he would go for the remaining unbearable days of his life until they got the answers they wanted. He knew the questions he would have to answer, always the same. *They are so sure they're going to crack me,* he thought.

They walked down the corridor and turned to the right. Turning right again, they stepped into a small room divided on one end, with heavy glass separating it from a hidden space behind. Because the Communists had designed the room for intimidation, a bright spotlight shone from a top corner of the far wall, hitting the metal chair where Arpad was motioned to sit. Before the light blinded him, he could see seated to his left the interrogating officer, who thumped his fingers impatiently on the hard surface. His lips curled off his teeth into a disgusted scowl, a permanent fixture. To Arpad's immediate right sat the interpreter, Major Kardos. This officer always spoke in Hungarian, translating the angry Czech's questions. Arpad thought he saw a hint of sympathy in this man's eyes, but under the nightmare of his current world, Arpad couldn't be sure. He glimpsed another man in civilian clothes sitting at the end of the table, but then the light hit Arpad straight in the eyes, blinding him to all but what his ears heard and the body odor he smelled.

IN HIS HANDS

"You are ready to tell the truth now," the interrogating officer said, his black club lying inches from his hands. "It's time to stop this nonsense. You are going to tell us who you were trying to smuggle out of Czechoslovakia." His voice was confident and reasoning. "You were found crossing our border with an empty compartment in the back of your Volkswagen van, obviously designed for smuggling. Clearly you had someone in mind when you tried to cross our border. Who was it?" He paused, his eyes narrowing.

"No one," Arpad answered.

"Who was it?" the officer yelled, his teeth snapping. "Was it someone you are trying to smuggle into the West?"

"I'm telling you the truth," Arpad said.

"You filthy liar. You are wasting our time. You will tell us." He thrust his club violently into Arpad's ribs and his voice lowered. "Or you'll be very sorry." He paused, his eyes boring into his prisoner.

Arpad knew the questions by heart, but still he must keep on his toes. One slight difference in answer, one simple variation, would indicate a lie. This is what they were looking for. The mental torture was designed so that he would make a slip, one little error, even if he didn't have a mistake to make. His captors were trained at this.

"There is no one, sir," Arpad said patiently. "I was only trying to pass through to Austria. I haven't been through Czechoslovakia for a long time and I thought I would take a different route than I usually do through Hungary."

"Do you have any relatives here?"

"No."

"Who are you in touch with?"

"Nobody." Arpad sighed.

"Why were you coming here with a van for smuggling?"

He explained the situation to the officer once more. How long he would be questioned, Arpad didn't know. He had to be completely honest so that a month from now he would

The Interrogation

still have the same answer, and no variations. The truth was the least dangerous option.

"I am running from the Romanian police for smuggling religious literature. I was trying to get my wife and myself into Austria to petition for political asylum. I was trying to smuggle her out of Hungary into Austria using my van. But then we saw a picture in the newspapers two days ago of a Volkswagen van like I owned. You can see for yourself if you get a copy of the *Budapest Times*. The van driver was caught trying to smuggle people in from Hungary to Austria like I was planning. This scared us, so we changed our plans. I decided to drive from Hungary through Czechoslovakia and then on to Austria. From there I planned to cross back to Yugoslavia with the van and smuggle her across from a different border crossing. I did mean to smuggle someone, but nobody from your country."

The officer, with white-knuckled fists, again stuck his club into Arpad's ribs, which were feeling rather bruised. "Stop lying. Do you know anyone from Czechoslovakia? Anyone at all?"

They already know the Union president, as he is watched closely by the government. I'll give them his name again, Arpad thought. "I met someone from here once when I was in Romania. He's the Union Conference president of the Seventh-day Adventist Church. He has nothing to do with my trip through your country, and I had no intentions of meeting him, nor of smuggling anybody into or out of your country."

"What's your profession?"

"I'm an Adventist pastor." *How many times must the man ask the same things?*

"How do we know you're an Adventist pastor? You must prove it. You will have to tell us what you believe." He looked at Arpad, seeming sure that Arpad would crumble under this line of questioning. "Can you do that?"

Arpad shrugged. "Certainly," he began. "I'd be happy to tell you. I believe first of all—"

"Wait." The officer held up his hand. "You must tell someone who knows. I don't want to hear about your worthless religion unless you are telling someone who is familiar with your faith." The Communist officer spat the words. He nodded to the man dressed in civilian clothes at the far end of the table. He turned back to Arpad. "Today we have with us a religion expert, a representative of the government. He is in charge of all religious matters in the country. He has some questions for you," the officer sneered. "He will determine if you are an Adventist pastor or not."

"Of course," Arpad replied. The Communist government didn't want to know about his religion. They couldn't care less. They were only looking for lies being told or for leads. This could prove a new direction in which to hunt.

The religion representative moved down the table to sit near Arpad. He was a thin man with dark hair and dark eyebrows, an intelligent eye, and the look of a scholar. He didn't carry the hostile, annoyed air of the interrogating officer.

"So, how does the government work with the Adventist Church in Romania these days?" he asked. The representative seemed genuinely interested in this information, as his job involved not only knowing about the religions practiced in his country, but included keeping track of how other Communist nations around them compared to their own. Arpad sensed that he was doing the man a favor. After some general questions about the Romanian church and politics, the representative picked out some questions that would separate Arpad from other Christians.

"What is the state of the dead?" the man asked.

"The Bible teaches that when there is no consciousness, there is no life. The 'spirit'—our breath—returns to God, but the spirit is not a conscious soul outside of our bodies. Death is like a sleep, and the righteous will rise at the second coming of Jesus," Arpad explained, trying to be concise.

"And hell?"

"The wicked will be raised in the judgment and consumed with fire, purging the earth of sin. With careful study, we under-

The Interrogation

stand that there is no everlasting hell. No man can quench it, but there will be an end. God will wipe all tears from our eyes."

The representative wrote something on his clipboard. "Are you a vegetarian?" he asked.

"Yes. It is one small part of living a healthier lifestyle. Not all Adventists are vegetarian, but most are known for not eating pork."

"Why don't you eat pork?" the man asked.

"It's a health issue," Arpad said. "We believe God asked the Israelites not to eat unclean meats for health reasons. Our church accepts this as another part of living healthfully, just as we refrain from smoking or drinking alcohol."

"I see," said the representative. "Can you tell me a little about the sanctuary?"

Arpad felt that he was running a mental gauntlet, but he found himself enjoying it at the same time. These were new questions. *He wants a short answer?* Arpad thought. *That will be tough.*

"God asked the Israelites to create a sanctuary," Arpad began. "The purpose of this was to use symbols to teach His people spiritual lessons. Two important symbols were the lamb and the priestly ministry."

"Can you explain?"

"The lamb was sacrificed as a substitute for our sins, and a symbol of Jesus' death on the cross for us. The high priest served as a mediator between the people and God, and once a year this priest went into the Most Holy Place to offer an atonement, or spiritual cleansing of the sanctuary. It represents the ministry that Jesus began doing for us after His death. Through Daniel 9, we understand that there is also a heavenly sanctuary, of which the earthly one was but an imitation. In Daniel 8 there is a prophecy of 2,300 days. A careful study of dates and history shows that everything has been fulfilled as predicted, exactly on time—Christ's birth, baptism, death, gospel to the world, and a final date that ended in 1844, the end of the prophetic period given. Here Christ entered the second and last part of His ministry, just as the high priest did in the Old Testament. This is called the investigative judgment, and shows to the universe who is worthy to be saved through Christ's sacrifice, both the dead in Christ and those now living. It shows the justice of God in saving those who believe in Jesus. It is being determined right now who is going to be ready for the resurrection and translation of His people when He comes again. He is a very fair God."

Arpad paused, wondering whether the man had understood a word. He felt as though he were preaching again. The representative simply wrote on his clipboard.

"So you believe in this rapture like all Christians do? One will be taken, another left? How do you explain that?" the representative asked.

He's still trying to find a way to test if I'm really an Adventist, thought Arpad. "We believe the rapture, or the Advent, is going to be such a worldwide, visible event that no one will miss it," said Arpad. "There is no secret rapture. That belief is dangerous because it allows many Christians to think there will be a second chance. There won't be."

"You worship on Sunday like other Christians do, right?"

"No." Arpad smiled. Didn't the very term *Seventh-day* Adventist explain this one?

"Why not?"

"Well, it's like this," he began. As he explained, he remembered another time, the time when he too had questioned his beliefs, the times he explained his beliefs to his high school principal. Arpad remembered his senior year in high school, when he finally understood the beauty of the Seventh-day Adventist message, the time when he had made his decision to follow Jesus for himself, aside from his parents' faith. The time when he no longer had doubts, when he first felt God's purpose for his life.

In fact, it had all come down to a matter of time—sacred time.

THE ARPAD SOO STORY

3

A Matter of Time

"That was an accurate explanation you made of the last chapters of Darwin's *Origin of Species,*" Director Tudor said, spinning his pointer in his fingers, turning to survey the notes Arpad had carefully detailed on the chalkboard. "Arpad, you've reviewed with us what Darwin argues about the evolution of man, that contemporary species arose from a selection of ancestors through a process of descent with modification. You're a good student at the top of your class, and you seem to understand natural selection and genetic variation thoroughly."

Arpad knew he wouldn't be let off the hook this easily. The principal of the high school, who was also the philosophy teacher, turned again to the students. "Arpad, you do agree with what you just told us, right?" Director Tudor's slow smile was a sign to the class that he was ready to pounce.

Arpad stood in front of his senior classmates. This was becoming a common occurrence, especially on Mondays after he had been absent from school on Saturday.

"No, Comrade Director, not in macro-evolution," Arpad re-

IN HIS HANDS

plied. The class tittered. They looked at their teacher and then at Arpad with anticipation.

"So, tell us, Arpad. Give us a diagram of how 'God' made the universe, of how he created you. Explain creation for us. Go ahead and explain it to the class. We'll take notes." He stood back, smirking.

"In the beginning God created the heavens and the earth," Arpad said, his voice strong. He was friends with his classmates and knew that no matter how hard the Communist teacher tried to humiliate him, his class would still be behind him.

" 'And the earth was without form and void—' "

"Right. Right," scoffed Director Tudor. "I know the Bible as well as you, Arpad. Skip that. How do you know that you were created? Prove it." He laughed. "Faith, is it?"

"You know about faith as well as I, Comrade Director. I think you need to have more faith to believe that this whole world just evolved in the universe, rather than accepting that God created everything," Arpad replied politely. "Whenever I am in a close relationship with God I can feel the positive effects of that relationship. I can feel the life-changing effects of that relationship in my life." He spoke with conviction. Holding his professor's gaze, he asked, "What does evolution do for you, Comrade Director?"

The class was silent.

"Well, I have proof that you haven't been created, that you are part of evolution. Just look at your monkey face." The class hooted. Director Tudor made a monkey face, hunched over, bobbed up and down, and scratched his armpits. The class roared. "Take your seat, Arpad. We can't spend all day on your special case. We need to spend some time now on political analysis. Class, take out your book by President Nicolae Ceausescu."* The students thumped out their heavy

---

* Pronounced Chowshesku.

A Matter of Time

books. Inside the cover of all the books, a picture of Ceausescu stared at each student.

The first and only president of Romania had written twenty-one volumes, which the Communist Party accepted and used in their government meetings and legislature. Students had to know these doctrines thoroughly. They were required to memorize portions of Ceausescu's speeches and be able to recite quotes from them when necessary. Arpad hated this. He was often called on to explain his views to the class, as his tended to differ. But Arpad learned Communism well. He felt that he must excel. The school would have no excuse to find fault with him in anything. Well, except for one thing—attendance.

In Romania, everyone worked or went to school for six days. Sunday was granted free, though seemingly not for religious reasons but because it was as good a day as any for a rest. The schools did not permit absences other than for medical reasons. Arpad's father, the Adventist minister, kept his mouth closed about Saturday school attendance in his church, an issue so big it had caused a split in his church. Some parents let their children go to school on Saturday because, of course, it was the law. And others kept their children home, facing the consequences. Sometimes this caused some church members to feel superior to others, depending on whether they kept their children home or not. Who was holier? Arpad's father, with agony, kept his voice silent and removed himself from the church's conflict. As an example, he let his own children decide for themselves what was right in their own conscience.

Though Arpad's childhood faith had been strong, a slow apathy had crept in, the result of always being expected to be a model child. In Romania, more so than in the United States, a church congregation watched and analyzed the pastor's children. When Arpad had reached junior high at the age of thirteen, he had rebelled, not claiming his parents' faith as his own. He wanted to be like his friends. He didn't want to be thought of as weird, so he grew indifferent to his parents' exhortations. His parents had allowed him to act on his own spiritual decisions. So until his senior year in high school Arpad had been interested in other things, and like many teenagers, had used religion only for social reasons.

Early in his senior year, Arpad heard that the president of the General Conference of Seventh-day Adventists would come from the United States and visit his father's tiny church on a Sabbath. He grew curious. *Why would such a "hot-shot" in the Adventist Church come here to the middle of nowhere?* He skipped school that Saturday morning and went to listen. For the first time in years, he truly listened. Unclouded by the indifference he usually felt when he heard his father preach, he suddenly began to understand the purpose of the Seventh-day Adventist Church, the reason for the hope that members claimed, and Arpad heard the voice of God speaking to his heart.

From that time forward Arpad began analyzing what he believed. With a vengeance he began to study for himself. No more of accepting things without question as he had done as a child. This was either a true faith, every bit of it, or he didn't want any part of it. As his conviction grew, the importance of keeping the seventh day as Sabbath struck a bulls-eye in his conscience. It was a sign between him and his Creator, an act of loyalty and love, an acknowledgement that God is God, obedience to a command that God had never changed. He made a commitment then that would threaten his future dreams. Though he was the only child in his family to so choose, Arpad would never again attend school on Saturday, God's hallowed memorial of Creation. Even if it cost him his diploma.

His father baptized Arpad in a large tin bathtub filled with well water in the church's courtyard, hidden from the street by a large wooden fence. The law forbade baptisms. The Communists reasoned that without evangelistic meetings, proselytizing of any kind, limited pastors, and restricted books and meetings, no one should ever reach the point of baptism. However, the more the government repressed Christianity, the more it grew. Communism didn't offer anything to most people, and for the Adventists, church was the highlight of their week. Since they were allowed only Sabbath to worship, the Adventists held worship services Friday evening and all day Saturday until sunset. It was during one of these services that his father baptized Arpad secretly in the big tub. But Arpad was too big to be completely immersed. Whenever his head was pushed down into the water, his feet would pop out. When his feet were pushed in, his head popped out. But he figured God would understand the situation. At the time there was no other way.

* * *

"What do you want to do after high school, Picu?" Arpad's classmate Feri Bozsodi asked another of their classmates. Feri was etching in calligraphy on smooth, white panes of glass. Picu was painting a large wooden map of Romania a bright green. Arpad stood behind the large frame that spread like a wall across the high school shop laboratory. He was wiring a light that would push through the board to the other side and light up the town of Ploiesti, where the Romanian poet Nichita Stanescu had been born.

"I don't know," Picu said. "I'd like to major in some kind of art. But since I didn't get to attend an art high school, I can't go on to study at an art university. I wouldn't mind being an engineer, or maybe I'll go into construction. Or maybe I'll paint houses—it can be quite intricate work, you know."

"If the job you're doing on Professor Rusu's map is even half of the talent you have," Arpad commented from behind the boards, "you'll be doing quite well for yourself." The three classmates worked two hours a week on this elective shop class after school. While some students did agriculture in the fields, carpentry, electronics, metal or woodworking, or tailoring in local shops, the three friends were given materials and guidance to help their homeroom teacher make a practical visual aid for his literature class.

Arpad was the leader and designer of this special project. The boys cut a huge map of Romania out of plywood. On the board they cut out holes for all the towns relating to famous Romanian authors and poets—their birthplaces, schools they attended, publications for which they worked, editorial positions for which they were active. From the control panel on the teacher's desk, Professor Rusu could pull a switch and the blue bulb for poet Mihai Eminescu would light up on the map. He would then push a button and a panel of transparent glass would light up, illuminating information about the publications Eminescu had written and other topics relating to the author's life. The display consisted of two large parts: a wooden map and a glass panel. Together these structures took the entire length of the front of the classroom. The map stood to the left, the panel, with its square grid, to the right. From his desk, using a control box, Professor Rusu would direct the stunning visual aid. As he lectured he would simply switch knobs and push buttons, and his class would take notes from the beautiful handwriting displayed on the lighted panels.

Arpad's design was Professor Rusu's pride. Already the school had put a lot of financial investment into this project. Representatives of the county department of education had come just the week before to interview Professor Rusu about his innovation and to congratulate his workers. The local county newspaper, *Steaua Rosie* (The Red Star) had printed an article about it. The accompanying photo showed the teacher standing beside the half-finished project, a proud smile on his face. This looked very good for the school, and as for Professor Rusu, he acted as though he had won a gold medal.

"What do you want to do, Arpad?" Feri asked. "Let me guess. Electronics? Carpentry? Plumbing? You could do anything.

A Matter of Time

You could even be a philosophy professor." At this the boys all laughed. "Professor Soo, could you explain natural selection and survival of the fittest again? I don't quite understand."

"Hey!" Arpad threw a small block of wood at his friend. "Stop that." Arpad laughed at his friends' jibes. He knew they would stand by him no matter what he believed.

"I am going to become a pastor."

Feri and Picu both paused in their work. Picu whistled. "You? You sure like to make things hard on yourself," Feri said. "The government is going to really like you now. Do you know the odds you're up against?"

"One in a thousand, probably much more than that."

"What do you mean?"

"To keep tight control over the spread of religion, the government only allows ten students every four years to go to the seminary. Because of this the standards of getting in are exceptionally high. I will have to take a rigorous test, get high recommendations from my church and also from church leaders at the top."

"How are you going to do that?" Feri asked. "Who's going to give you the recommendations for that? I've known you for quite a while and you're no saint. If they knew about all the times we've had—"

"I know," Arpad cut in. "But I've really given my life to God now. Things are different for me. They will see it. God will provide a way."

His friends looked uncomfortable. They were young Communists—atheists— even if Arpad was not. It had been drilled into them from childhood.

Arpad shrugged. "Besides this, there are hundreds of applicants for the ministry. I figure the odds are pretty strong against me. It will be a miracle."

"What will be the real miracle is your graduating from high school," Picu warned. "What's with skipping school every Saturday? You're going to be thrown out before you pass the high school exit exam, or any seminary entrance exam. It's just a matter of time. Why can't you just attend for the rest of the year? Your tenth-grade sister does. You've come this far. How can you ruin these plans with this stupidity? You never used to care."

"Professor Rusu will be so disappointed," Feri added. "You know how much of his pride is in each of those light bulbs you're wiring. We couldn't finish this project without you."

Arpad sighed. It was hard to be the only child of the family who wouldn't go to school on Saturday. His brother and sisters acknowledged the same religion, but they didn't seem to care about the day, just as he had not before. "It's just something that I can't do anymore. My conscience won't let me. I'll just have to take the consequences."

Feri and Picu shook their heads in amazement. "Say goodbye to the seminary. You'd make a better electrician or plumber. You'd probably get yourself arrested as a pastor since you're always doing or saying something a bit too risky."

"Yeah, you're probably right," Arpad said, going back behind the map to hook up more light bulbs. The rest of the hour they worked in silence.

Arpad knew that he wanted more than anything to become a pastor. He had felt God's call so strongly that he had no doubt. It was a quiet conviction that filled his whole soul. Romania needed Adventist pastors desperately. They were retiring thirty to forty pastors every four years, but only letting ten new pastors into the ministry every four years. The government wanted the Church to die off. Although there were hundreds applying for these ten positions, Arpad knew he had to try. He had already begun the arduous application process. It would take a miracle.

"God, if this is Your purpose for me, help me to graduate," he prayed. "I'm keeping Your Sabbath, but I don't know how long I will be allowed to remain in school with all these unex-

A Matter of Time

cused absences. Your will be done." Arpad continued to hope and pray. He continued to skip school every Saturday.

The month of this conversation, Arpad was absent four times, and he knew that his private decision would soon be a public one. One doesn't get sick every Saturday, and Director Tudor didn't wait long. This was a political fault, especially because it was for religious reasons. The school needed to educate Arpad out of weakness and turn him into a young Communist.

Director Tudor challenged Arpad continually in philosophy class. "Why do you have to keep the Sabbath when the entire world doesn't keep it?" Director Tudor asked. "It's a Jewish custom. It has absolutely nothing to do with Christianity."

" 'By the seventh day God had finished the work He had been doing, so on the seventh day He rested from all His work. And God blessed the seventh day and made it holy, because on it He rested from all the work of creating that He had done,' " Arpad quoted. "Adam wasn't a Jew. Adam was man. Adam is the father of the entire human race. It became a Jewish tradition, but it is not based on that. It has absolutely nothing to do with Jewish tradition, just like marriage doesn't have anything to do with Jewish tradition. God made man and woman and put them together and married them," he told his professor. "Because you are married to your wife, does that mean that you are Jewish?"

The class laughed. They didn't know their Bible as well as Arpad, nor as well as Director Tudor. The professor frowned. Though he loved to mock others, he did not like to be mocked.

Their discussions would stop, but Director Tudor would continually bring the subject up again on other days. Still, Arpad had a reason for everything.

"Why do you not eat pork, then?" Professor Tudor tried a different angle. "That's a Jewish law? Why do you not keep the rest of the Jewish laws too?"

"God gave His people health rules because He knows exactly what is the best for us to eat. Look at the Egyptians, for example. God promised the people who obeyed His rules that none of the sicknesses that were in Egypt would have an effect on them. He knew exactly what they needed in the washing of hands, ceremonial, and health laws. That's why today the Jewish people are healthier than most other nations. You go anywhere in the world today and the statistics will tell you this. Eating 'clean' meat is a lifestyle issue, one that our church has accepted. It is not one of the Ten Commandments. It is one of the health laws that we believe can still benefit us today."

"Humph."

The next class period Arpad brought in an article from a secular publication that showed how bad it is from a health perspective to eat nonkosher meat. The professor didn't have much to say. He would always try to humiliate Arpad in front of his classmates, but Arpad felt that the curse had turned into a blessing. He felt even closer to his classmates than before.

The next Saturday Arpad was missing again.

On Monday Director Tudor told Arpad, "Come see me in my office after school." Arpad knew that the time had come. His stomach lurched. He had rehearsed this moment in his mind, but he wasn't ready.

Director Tudor's office was large and foreboding. A heavy wooden desk dominated the middle of the room. Behind the desk a large portrait of President Ceausescu glared at Arpad, as pictures of the president did in every hallway and inside every textbook cover. To the right by a window hung a huge Romanian flag. Thick hardbound volumes of Communist lore and philosophy lined the shelves around the office. Director Tudor leaned back in his large, black leather chair with his fingers pressed together in an upside-down V. He tapped them together. Professor Rusu, who also served as the assistant principal, sat on an opposite chair. He looked irritated, and a worried expression lined his face.

A Matter of Time

Director Tudor cleared his throat. "Arpad, your attendance record shows that you are missing five Saturdays in a row." His eyebrows knit together, frowning. "You cannot possibly have health problems this consistently. School is not a matter of religion. It's a matter of politics. Your country must come first. You are choosing to spit upon the education your country has so generously provided." He stood up from his chair and walked to the window.

"Education is not a right, Arpad," he continued. "It is a gift, a privilege. You do not have to be here, and you are choosing to skip school every week." He turned to face Arpad, a firm look in his eyes. "If you have one more absence from school, we are going to expel you from school. Is that clear?"

Arpad took a deep breath. His knees felt weak. He wanted to say, "OK," but it wasn't easy to ask for the flames. He cast a silent prayer upward.

"You can kick me out of the school, but I am still not going to come on Saturday, my Sabbath, because my relationship with God and what I feel toward Him is a lot more important to me than what you want me to become. I know you are trying to educate me out of this, but I am not going to become a Communist. Even if I did, I would become the worst one." Arpad sighed. "You wouldn't want me anyway."

"Take your books and don't come back. You are no longer a student here," growled Director Tudor. "Get out of my sight. You bring shame on this school. You are not worthy to belong to this school. You bring shame on your country." That was the worst insult a young patriot could receive, and all students were indoctrinated in patriotism. Professor Rusu's face looked pale. Arpad quietly took his book bag from where it rested on the floor. Feri was right. So much for being a pastor. *God, where are You when I need You?* His heart hurt. A lump formed in his throat. Professor Rusu covered his face with a hand and exhaled. Director Tudor turned his back as Arpad shut the door behind him.

31

The Furnace

"What do You have for me now?" Arpad prayed. He had been reading about Shadrach, Meshach, and Abednego, the three Hebrew friends in the Bible who defied the king's command and refused to kneel before the golden idol. They had survived being thrown into a fiery furnace and a divine being had appeared with them there. "I've been thrown in the fiery furnace, but I'm not sure I see You with me," Arpad continued. "Are You here? I wanted to work for You, but now it feels as though my dreams are over. How can I ever go back to school and graduate if I refuse to go to school on Saturday? I've been praying and praying. I don't know what You want me to do now." Arpad stayed home for a few days, talking over the situation with his parents. His father, despite the bleak outlook for his son, looked proud.

"Just wait," his father said. "Jesus says that we are blessed when we are persecuted for righteousness' sake. Something good will turn up."

"If what I feel right now is a blessing, I'm not sure I want

The Furnace

it," Arpad said. "They're not really persecuting me for religious reasons, are they? It's just the law."

"A law that wants you to follow it above the law of God," his father replied. "By your actions you are showing who is more important in your life: God or Ceausescu. I don't think you will regret it."

Several days had inched by since Arpad had been thrown out of school. Gabriella, his younger sister, came home from school one afternoon with a message.

"Professor Rusu wants to see you tomorrow morning at seven-thirty," she said. "He didn't tell me why."

When Arpad walked into Professor Rusu's office the next morning, the homeroom teacher smiled broadly, looking up from his lesson-plan book. "Arpad, I had to fight for you," he said. "It wasn't easy, but you are accepted back into school on one condition. You must finish the map project by the end of the year."

"Really?" Arpad exclaimed, his heart doing a cartwheel.

"It was a tough case, but we decided to overlook your Saturday problem only if you give us an outstanding final product. We have invested so much time and money in this, and if you are gone it will not be completed. Do I have your promise?"

"Yes!" Arpad vowed. "Don't worry, Professor Rusu. *The Red Star* will have another updated article about your ingenious innovation by the time school is out. It will be so wonderful that all the teachers from other high schools will visit you to model it for their schools. You will be famous. I won't let you down."

Professor Rusu beamed. "Good. I'll see you in class."

Every spare second Arpad worked on the map. He spent extra hours every day after school wiring the lights and switches, taking care of every detail to make it perfect. Feri and Picu worked with him. They knew what was at stake.

IN HIS HANDS

"That was a close one, Arpad," Picu said. "If you live your life testing fate like that, I don't know what will become of you. Professor Rusu pulled you out of this one, but he won't be able to pull you through your exit exams."

"God used Professor Rusu to answer my prayers," said Arpad humbly. "The exit exams are in God's hands too. We've just got to get this map done."

"Right," Feri said wryly. "I don't have to agree with you on your religious beliefs to be your friend, and we don't have much time till the end of year. Do you want help on Sunday?" Arpad smiled. *What true friends,* he thought.

The Baccalaureates. Arpad cringed at the thought. Only those who passed the infamous tests had a chance of going on to the university—the seminary in his case. He had to pass five tests: the Romanian oral and written tests, the math oral and written tests, and then take another test on a subject of the student's choice. For his elective, Arpad had chosen biology. By now he knew his evolutionary theory quite well. These tests lasted anywhere from seven to ten days. If any of Arpad's tests were scheduled on Saturday, he wouldn't be able to complete these and, consequently, he wouldn't be able to graduate. Rescheduling was not an option.

Arpad opened his test schedule gingerly, praying. His heart sank. Sure enough, his oral Romanian test was scheduled for Saturday morning.

I have lost everything, Arpad mourned, again sick at heart. *Why did I come back to school and work so hard for this, if it doesn't even matter now? God, I'm going to trust You on this one because there's nothing I can do. I'll study for them anyway.* On Friday, he took the Romanian written exam and felt that he had done well but not spectacularly. His written-exam score would be multiplied by his oral-exam score to give him the final grade. But 80 percent times zero was still zero. He went to church on Sabbath, and when the Romanian oral test was

The Furnace

given, he was the only one from his class who wasn't there. No one else would think of missing it.

Arpad's biology exam was scheduled for Sunday morning. He awakened early. *It won't make any difference,* he thought. *But I want to finish what I've started, for the principle of the thing, even though I'll have to retake all the tests again next year because I failed one.* Arpad opened the door of the administration building, expecting the hallway to be quiet except for the students waiting for the biology exam. Instead, the hallway where the exams were going to take place hummed with more students than he had expected. Arpad walked past a group of students waiting outside the door of the oral exam room. "What are you doing here?" Arpad asked. "The Romanian oral exam was yesterday."

"They didn't get to all the 'S's' yet," a classmate replied. "We have to finish up today. Hey, you're an S. Didn't you know this?"

"'No!" Arpad said. "I had no idea. You're kidding me! This never happens!"

Professor Rusu appeared down the hall. He saw Arpad, and relief filled his face. "Arpad, come here," he said urgently. "They didn't get to the 'S's' yesterday. You're going to be OK. Are you ready to take the oral exam right now?"

Arpad's heart warmed. *Even though Professor is a very strong Communist leader, he is still on my side,* he thought.

"Sure." Arpad had never been more ready.

Then it was graduation day. Arpad and his fellow classmates lined up to receive their diplomas, handed to them by Director Tudor. When Arpad's turn came, the surly Communist leader shook his hand and then, to Arpad's surprise, gave him a hug.

"I'm proud of you, Arpad," he said. "You were a very good student."

Even Communist leaders have human sympathy and emotions, Arpad realized. *This man was only doing his duty.*

35

* * *

"What do you think? Is he an Adventist?" asked the interrogating officer.

This man, too, is only doing his duty, Arpad thought after being interrogated by the Czech representative of religious matters. Arpad had answered the questions put to him as thoroughly as possible.

"Yes, he's definitely an Adventist," the representative replied. "As you can see, he could easily be a pastor." He smiled. "He doesn't have a problem talking."

The guard led Arpad back to his cell. The hours beat mercilessly inside him for several more days, turning his emotions black and blue. He had been in hopeless situations before, but this was the grand finale. *By my actions, even though I was trying to help people, I have taken away the possibility of ever being useful as a minister.* This echoed through his heart constantly. *My poor wife. She was so courageous, and now they will send her back to Romania to be in jail as well. All because of me. I feel completely deserted. Lord, why did You let this happen? I worked so hard, so long, with dedication. What are You trying to teach me?*

The jail door smashed open again. The interrogating warden stalked in with Kardos, the interpreter.

"The Hungarians have come asking us to release you to them. It is against the law for us to do this. We must send you back to Romania, your home country. Do you think we should send you back? Are you ready to tell us the truth?" Giving prisoners back to their own country was what countries did for each other.

"I can't answer that," Arpad said, dejected. "That's what I would expect to happen." *At least they will know I am telling the truth.*

"Of course that will happen. Unless you tell us who it is you were trying to smuggle out of Czechoslovakia." Again the club bruised Arpad's ribs. *Then they will keep me jailed in Czechoslovakia.* Arpad finished the unspoken truth in his mind.

"There is no one," Arpad replied. *Stop. Go away.* The questions, the mental torture never seemed to end. Nor did the waiting for the inevitable. This continual barrage of questions drove him crazier than the inactivity inside his cell. Once before he had waited, but then he had had a future ahead of him.

The cell door slammed shut. Left alone with the spider in the window, Arpad's thoughts returned to his homeland.

Waiting

"Any word yet?" Feri had asked Arpad. "You better start making other plans because you probably won't make the cut for seminary."

Waiting in Romania was a fact of life. Nothing happened quickly, it seemed, especially for eighteen-year-old Arpad. Now that he had graduated from high school, he had to wait to see if he would be accepted into the seminary. Every reference in his life had to be questioned, every questionable action in his life or flaw in his character evaluated.

The Church had too much to lose if they made one poor choice in the chosen ten. These seminary students would have a huge responsibility resting upon them, and if one dark spot existed in the past, it could hold too much risk for the future. The future of church growth and leadership rested heavily on this little band. Each graduating pastor would have the responsibility of caring for five to six little churches in a district. He would have to drive a long way every weekend. There wouldn't be much support financially or emotionally. It was a serious profession to want to enter.

Waiting

Will the seminary check into all the years before I was baptized? Maybe they will find something crazy I did and not allow me in, Arpad worried. He checked the mail every day, and one day the notice arrived. He had passed the entrance exam and was accepted. Arpad was filled with joy. The long wait had been worth it.

"I won't let You down, Lord," he promised, knowing what a privilege he had just received. He moved to Bucharest, the capital city of Romania with a population of two million, and dived into his studies. The seminary students were assigned to work with local pastors and their churches on the weekend to gain practice. Arpad loved the seminary and felt continually thankful that he had been given his dream.

One day in his first quarter the dean and Romanian union president, Elder Dumitru Popa, called him to their office.

"Arpad, I'm afraid I have some bad news for you," Elder Popa said. "Something has surfaced in your past that could be a serious character issue against your name. This is a huge concern because of the shortage of pastors in Romania. Churches don't want to take chances on funding someone about whom they have any concerns." Elder Popa's face crinkled in sympathy.

Arpad gulped. His mind raced to all the times in his past when he possibly could have done something serious. He had always been rather a rascal, he hadn't always kept the Sabbath, and he hadn't always had a relationship with God, but surely this wouldn't keep him back now? He had never done anything serious to damage his character reputation. He listened as Elder Popa continued.

"A certain family from a church your father used to pastor a little while ago has come to tell us that you had inappropriate contact with a girl, that on a camping trip a few years ago, you took her inside your tent. Is this true?"

"What? Of course not!" Arpad was indignant. "I don't know what you're talking about." He racked his brain. *Who would* say such a thing? For what reason? Where could they have dug up this crazy accusation?

Suddenly the reason dawned on him. "I think I have an idea of where this came from, and I promise it isn't true. You see, there were several girls." He blushed. "I mean, please, let me explain what really happened and defend my character."

"Go ahead."

"When I was fifteen there was a family in the church whose daughter really wanted to be my girlfriend. I wasn't interested in her, and I didn't respond to her advances. However, her parents were the only ones who had a car, and they would ask me to go ice-skating with them a ways away on a pond that was excellent for skating. I would, and when I skated with their daughter, I held her hand. That was the extent of our contact and the 'relationship.'

"One day friends from Hungary came to visit me, and we all went camping together. It was a youth camp with many other people from the church. This girl's family was along. My friends and I met some other girls from another village there, and we hung out with them. We went hiking together, and that evening we all got together in a big tent to play games. I was never alone with any girl in a tent, and nothing inappropriate happened.

"Now the parents of the girl who wanted to date me are spreading lies about me because they are angry that I didn't date their daughter. What can I do to convince everyone that I didn't do anything wrong?"

"I'm sorry, Arpad, but this is a serious charge. We will have to go back to the church board of this village and talk with them," Elder Popa said. "You probably will have to leave Bucharest to come with us to give your testimony."

The girl's family had a strong influence in the church board, Arpad discovered, and he found that even three years after the event in question, the board was biased against him.

Waiting

The seminary leaders even hunted down the others who had come on that camping trip with him and the other families in the group. They all supported him. "No, there is nothing wrong with his character. We never saw this kind of thing happening," they confirmed. Still the family felt wronged, and with their church members, continued to complain about Arpad attending the seminary.

Again Elder Popa called him into his office. Arpad could tell that he seemed uncomfortable and sad. Elder Popa sighed and asked Arpad to sit down.

"What's wrong?" asked Arpad. "Did you hear something else about my character from three years ago?" He sat down in the chair in front of the president's large desk.

"No," said Elder Popa, choosing his words with care. "But the faculty of the seminary and I feel that the best way to calm the church down will be for you to pull back from the seminary for a while. We will allow you to re-enroll after things have quieted down."

"Pull back from the seminary? What do you mean? That will be another four years from now. It was so hard to get in, and I've already started. That's not fair." Arpad jumped to his feet, his fists clenched.

"Listen, Arpad," Elder Popa continued. "You are only eighteen, the youngest student ever to enroll in our seminary. There are twenty-eight-year-old students who are only beginning. Waiting a few more years will not hurt you."

"But four more years. That seems a lifetime."

"It is not an order, but a suggestion." Arpad put his face in his hands.

"We do have some positive news though," Elder Popa said. "We feel that the Communist government is loosening up on their enrollment policy and that within two years we will be able to enroll another ten students. You would only have to wait for two years. We will look forward to seeing you again, and you will have a fresh start. You won't have to retake the entrance exam. Think about it. You could fight this, but I hope you will take our advice."

Arpad thought and thought. *I feel like Joseph in the Bible who was thrown to the dungeon when he hadn't done anything wrong. But if the faculty thinks it is best that I not be here right now, I should probably take their suggestion.* Two years still seemed like a long time. "OK," Arpad said finally. "If you think it is best."

Arpad's father had moved to pastor in the town of Oradea, a town near the Romanian border with Hungary. Arpad returned to live with his family. He came to gain a lot of practical experience working for the church, and he was treated like a youth pastor. During this time he also sold life insurance beside the border patrol station and listened to many stories of how smugglers and illegal aliens would get caught, shot, or returned to their countries for harsh imprisonment. He listened wide-eyed to the stories the police would tell each other outside his little sales booth. What time he didn't spend helping at the church or selling insurance, he spent working as a plumber. *I'm wasting my time,* he thought. *I could be half way done with my seminary education right now but instead I'm installing people's pipes.* "I don't know how this could be a part of Your plan, Lord," he prayed, "but I sure am ready to start my real work for You."

The Strategy

After pressing the government year after year for more students, the Adventist Church succeeded in winning government approval for increased enrollment in the seminary. "We are allowed to practice our religion, but we aren't allowed to expand or organize," the Church leaders had pointed out. "It will be worse for the government if we don't have more pastors. The churches will not die off with no one to guide them as the government desires, but rather the congregations will continue to grow with lay members leading, but with less order. It will be easier for the government to control an organized church than an unorganized one."

The government finally accepted this reasoning, and two years later as promised, Arpad was readmitted with nine others into the seminary. The commotion about his past was forgotten. He became completely involved in his seminary duties and made friends easily.

He and his seminary classmates, in order to share the workload, typed up their course notes between them. One typed up Adventist Church history, another homiletics, another Romanian church history, another counseling. They also typed up Sabbath School lessons and other manuscripts. They typed the notes on thin white paper, putting carbon between the sheets, and made up to ten carbon copies each time. Remembering his childhood days working with his father in bookbinding, Arpad started binding his and his classmates' notes and lessons.

In Romania the Communist government ordered all the typewriters to be registered yearly so that any printed material found could be immediately traced back to the typewriter's owner. All mechanical typewriters were unique, like a fingerprint. Certain letters were hit harder, higher, or lower on the line. Printing material for course work on campus wasn't an issue, but taking them outside of the school's perimeters was illegal. The law allowed for printing some Sabbath School lesson copies, but the amount allowed was enough for only half of the Church members in the nation. No songbooks had been allowed to be published since 1949, especially songs with music notes. The books of the well-known Adventist author, Ellen White, were forbidden as well. Anyone who wanted could have a Bible, but the cost of a Bible was as much as some people earned in a month. Many groups were already involved in smuggling Bibles. Arpad saw the hunger of the church for Adventist literature. Was there nothing he could do, he wondered?

One day when Arpad and two of his closest seminarian friends were walking to class, he brought up the subject. "Listen," he confided, his voice growing soft. He pulled out a Sabbath School lesson quarterly. "Can you keep a secret?"

"Of course," his friends promised.

"Can we trust each other with our lives?" His friends stopped walking.

"Arpad, what did you get yourself into this time?" Mihai Baciu, his roommate, said with a laugh.

"This is serious," Arpad said. He pulled them off the sidewalk and under a small grove of trees nearby. "Here, take a

The Strategy

look at this." He flicked through the pages of the quarterly and handed it to Mihai.

"It's a lesson study, Arpad. What's your point?"

"How many of them do we have access to?"

"Only a few. You know that. That's why we type them up and take them to the bindery."

"Right, but what would happen if every church member had one across Romania?" Arpad made a wide sweep with his hands. "There are hungry churches with everyone zealous to study. Do you know how much they would appreciate buying this little copy?"

Jakab Treitly, the other friend, nodded. "It's true, but that's the way it's always been. There aren't enough to go around."

"I know," Arpad continued, "but we have access to them. How can we not do something about it? Don't you ever feel that you aren't doing enough?"

"Well sure, Arpad," said Mihai. "You know as well as I do what the consequences are for this, Arpad. It's illegal. First of all, there's no way we could type more copies than we are typing already, and these only supply us here at the seminary. Second, we would need to print them at a shop. Fat chance of that ever happening. And third, if the seminary got wind of this we would be kicked out." He thumped Arpad on the shoulder. "Pastors are too valuable to take these kinds of risks. You know how hard it was for us to get accepted in the seminary."

Jakab jumped in. "There are government informants inside the seminary as well as anywhere you go around the town. Any of our rooms could be bugged, and especially our faculty's offices and homes. Someone would find out and talk. If you're caught with more than one or two Sabbath School lessons outside of this campus, you're going to be sauerkraut in prison. If the government catches anyone smuggling, it's five to twenty-five years." His whisper grew hoarse and loud. "Up to twenty-five years, Arpad."

IN HIS HANDS

"I know, I know," Arpad said, nodding. "Believe me, I've thought through all these reasons in my head. But I can't help thinking of all the people who want to study, who depend only on their pastor, if they're lucky enough to have one, only one weekend a month. Aren't they worth the risk? The message needs to spread to the entire world. Our little country sure is having a hard time hearing it. I can't sit back when people are starving for what I have and the power is in my grasp. I didn't come to the seminary to sit around when I have this chance."

"How so, Arpad? What chance?" asked Mihai. "How are you going to print that many copies? How are you going to smuggle the amount you're talking of around the country? You're crazy."

"I know, but you haven't heard my plan yet. We've been typing up our notes for a while now, and you know that bookbinder where we take our class notes? I'm getting to be rather good friends with him. He does a good job binding for us, and he's a trustworthy guy. I can tell."

"How can you tell?"

Arpad pointed to the Sabbath School quarterly still in Mihai's hands. "You're holding it. This was printed on the Communist Army Press. It's not the original."

Both friends stared. "But it looks exactly like it," Jakab said. "How can this be? And on the Army press? How did it get printed in there? There's no way!"

"I've told you," Arpad said. "My friend is good. Very good. And he's already been printing hundreds of them. He's been smuggling the quarterlies in and out of the press in his book bag. He smuggles the printing in page by page. He takes it apart, reprints it, and binds it back. I don't know how he does it exactly, because we don't talk about it and I don't meet with him much now that he's doing this. I think he must do his bookbinding there after hours. Then he smuggles ten or twenty out when he leaves at night. He passes guards daily,

The Strategy

but no one checks his bag if he doesn't carry very many. The books add up every day. He lives in a fourth-floor flat in the Militari area. Each time I have gone to pick up the small packet, I make a couple of rounds, enter through different entrances, and hide for a while before sneaking to his apartment to be sure that nobody follows me. He's very cautious. So am I."

"But the government has instant searches inside the press," Mihai exclaimed. "The government controls everything in a press, especially in their Army press. That's one way they suppress communication and rebellion. Printing is the biggest danger for them. Don't you think they're watching for this kind of thing? If anyone suspects or follows this bookbinder and catches him, he will blame you. That's prison for him and for you, five, ten, maybe twenty-five years," he reminded.

"It's a high risk," Arpad agreed. "He's taking a tremendous risk. But he's getting paid very well. He was not making a whole lot of money before, and he's getting paid more money now than he could ever make on his own. I have confidence in him."

Jakab raised his eyebrows. "Since when have you had money to start an operation like this, Arpad? You're a seminary student. Where did you get this money? Are you practicing thievery as well?"

"Come on," Arpad said, "I know people. Some very dedicated church members from here loaned me the money to put up front, and when the books sell, they'll get their money back. Illegal books are very expensive, but they will be bought. Even though Adventists are persecuted here, they are very hard workers. Many of them go into the best businesses or are entrepreneurial, so they are doing well. God has blessed them. Even if they are poor, they will save up that money from anywhere to buy the book." Both friends nodded. They knew this was true.

"So you're going to smuggle more than quarterlies, even books?"

Arpad nodded. "We have to start small. But soon it will be *Steps to Christ, The Desire of Ages,* and then hymnals. Can't you see the churches thriving now? No more penciled stanzas for the choirs. There will be spiritual food for struggling members. They will know Jesus as a closer Friend than ever before. The government can't stop God."

"Did you say 'we'?" questioned Jakab. "Arpad, are you asking what I think you're asking?"

"Of course." Arpad grinned.

Mihai still looked dazed. "This is absolutely crazy," he said. "And you think you can do all of this on your own?" His friend nudged him in the ribs, already ahead of him.

"No, I need your help, both of you. Will you help me?"

Both friends were quiet, thinking of their future, uneasy about stepping onto a swaying bridge across an abyss. The late fall breeze ruffled the pages of the quarterly Mihai held in his hands. Other classmates passed them on the sidewalk a few yards away, oblivious to the question Arpad had posed that would change these three friends' lives forever.

"Do you have a plan for how we're going to smuggle these quarterlies, these libraries around the country?" Mihai asked after a long pause. "It's going to take a lot of strategy."

THE ARPAD SOO STORY

7

Black Market

Arpad picked up the small brown briefcase from the fourth-story apartment. He mentally weighed its contents. It wouldn't be noticeably heavy. Looking around quickly, he walked down the stairs and went several blocks to the tram station. He boarded the yellow electric tram and rode through the dark city to the train station, where he would wait for the evening ride at nine o'clock. Chill wind blew in Arpad's face, but he kept warm in his thick sheepskin coat.

That wasn't bad tonight, he thought, looking at the people lounging on the station benches nearby, bags in hand. He hadn't seen any of their faces before, and no one looked away into a newspaper when he glanced at them. *No one looks suspicious yet,* he thought with a sigh of relief, but he couldn't be too sure. Arpad always took a different way to the train station. Sometimes he went by taxi; sometimes he got a ride in a friend's car. Sometimes he even walked the long distance, always making sure he varied the times and transportation so he wouldn't establish a pattern. If anyone followed him, he had to be alert so he could get rid of the briefcase and disappear.

IN HIS HANDS

The train rushed into the station, squealing to a halt, and the gush of air from the hot engine puffed Arpad's hair from his face. He boarded the fourth car in front of him, lifted the briefcase onto the rack above the chairs, and sat down nearby on a hard seat. There were seven other seats in his compartment, and only two were taken. Avoiding anyone's eyes, he turned to the window and watched the old buildings of Bucharest slip by outside the glass. Several stations later, near the edge of the city, his friend Mihai boarded the car, his tall frame filling the doorway. He sat three chairs down on the opposite side. Arpad continued looking out the window, not acknowledging his presence. At the next station, Arpad got out, leaving the briefcase on the rack above under the watchful care of Mihai. No one in the car would know if he were just taking a break to smoke in the aisle, or to visit someone else. If the police were to come by, as they often did, pointing at baggage in the racks for the owner to open it, the briefcase would go unclaimed. No one could accuse Mihai of owning the briefcase because he hadn't brought it in.

Mihai would watch the briefcase until another station when Jakab would walk in, strolling through the cars to find a seat nearby. Mihai would exit, leaving the briefcase under his unacknowledged friend's eye. The next morning when the train got to Brasov, Jakab would then unload it, and he would be approached by a church member who was waiting with a car to redistribute the material through local smuggling chains to the surrounding churches. The delivery was prepaid, and because the people, routes, and times always varied, there was never a noticeable pattern—nothing that could be recognized as suspicious.

Jakab and Mihai weren't the only smugglers involved. Soon there were different people assigned to different routes to five major cities around Romania. The chain slowly grew to twenty, thirty, forty people, Arpad never knew how many for sure. He left the distribution chain to trusted people from

Black Market

the villages. His responsibility was to make the arrangements, get the books printed, and then get them out of the city safely. When they traveled to major cities, the smugglers would often buy prearranged tickets. The next person in the chain at another station would know to look for Car C, Row 18. He would walk in, casually take the briefcase and go to his own car, or else sit down nearby. All the details were carefully prearranged down to the exact time of train arrival and description of the luggage. No one knew exactly who was at what station, but when they recognized one of the team members, they would leave. The team had to use a secret code when talking on any phone or in conversation, and everyone knew that north really meant west and six lei (the Romanian currency) really meant six o'clock. "Bad weather" meant bad news. The hub city of Iasi* really meant Craiova.

Day by day, Arpad's smuggling team perfected their mission. One major accomplishment of which Arpad and his friends were proud was creating a songbook. Two talented musician pastors, Orban and Faluvegy, put all the notes together for a 280-page book. Because every church had a choir, these books sold very well. For almost twenty years they had been using handwritten notes, painstakingly reproduced.

Arpad picked up the literature from the bookbinder every day and hid it in different places—storage units, people's homes, attics, and basements—and then he and his friends spread them around the country. Sometimes people came to Bucharest to pick up a large quantity of books. This was more dangerous because heavy luggage usually got searched. Sometimes Arpad asked church members from northern Romania to come down with a car or pickup truck with strong support in the back. On the bed of the truck, they would hide these books in small boxes, so they wouldn't be evident. Too much

---
* Pronounced Yashi.

contraband would make the loaded truck sag, and sagging vehicles were usually stopped and searched. Even putting two suitcases in the back of a car would weigh the car down enough to be pulled over.

Toward the end of Arpad's second year in the seminary, his friend Mihai bought a red Dacia,* a small Romanian car, modeled after the French Renault 12. He was the first seminarian to own a car. Though no students could leave the seminary without permission, Arpad and his friends decided to sneak off with a load of literature to take up to Bacau, a northern city where Mihai lived. At the bottom of the trunk they placed *Steps to Christ* and the hymnals. With each book, the little car sank lower and lower. After the students had crammed in almost 2,000 books, they packed their seminary course books on top. They had several drop-off spots along the way, trying to make Bacau by nightfall.

In the town of Roman, their last stop before Bacau, they were approaching a busy intersection when a blue and white police car pulled out behind them, its siren wailing.

"Start praying," said Mihai. "He saw the trunk."

Arpad took one look at Mihai in the driver's seat and closed his eyes. Tightlipped, Mihai pulled the Dacia over by the curb. They knew the officer had seen the heavy sag, even though there were fewer books in it now than when they had started. The police officer, dressed in a blue uniform and matching cap, strode to Mihai's window.

"License and registration, please," he snapped. Then he asked to see the brake lights, headlights, and turn signals. "Where are you going?" he asked, abrupt and cold. "What do you have in your trunk?"

"We're students," Mihai said. "Since it's almost the end of the year, we are taking some of our stuff home to Bacau."

"Let's see what you have. Open the trunk."

---

* Pronounced Duchia.

Mihai got out and led the officer to the back and unlocked the trunk. The officer saw the copies of homiletics and books on New Testament exegesis on the top. "What are these?" he asked, picking one up.

"These are our course books," Mihai said. In the front, Arpad clenched his eyes, furiously mouthing his prayer.

The officer started poking around, removing more books. "There's a lot here," he said.

"We've studied a lot, officer. Those are our textbooks too."

"How come there are so many of the same book?" he asked, his eyes narrowing. Arpad held his breath. Mihai's vague explanation didn't satisfy the officer. "Open it up. Take everything out so I can see it," the officer ordered. Mihai slowly took some books out until the officer began ripping them out himself and piling them on the pavement. *Stop!* Arpad wanted to yell. *Go away!*

"Lord," Arpad prayed, "please do something to take his attention off us. Please!" It would soon be all over. He felt the sweat collecting on his face and heard Mihai's voice, trying to stay calm, and the officer's terse reply. Mihai's face looked worse than it did when he had eaten bad cafeteria food. The pile of books on the pavement continued to grow.

Hungry People

"This is it," Arpad prayed, his heart in his throat, "unless You save us. Please send a distraction," he pleaded. He leaned back in his seat and waited.

Vrrrooom. A black Volga, a large Russian car, the largest made during the seventies, roared through the red light at the intersection a few feet away. The oncoming lanes of cars screeched to a stop, some swerving in the intersection to miss the speeder, and the honking began.

The police officer looked up, cursed, threw the license and registration into the trunk, ran to the police car, jumped in, started the siren, and took off, following the Volga.

Arpad leaped out of the car and joined Mihai, and they dropped to their knees right there on the pavement.

"Thank You, Lord!" they prayed, their hearts flooding with praise. Arpad felt lightheaded with joy. Then they threw the books back into the trunk and sped off so that if the cop decided to come back they would be long gone.

They made it safely to Bacau, dropped off the rest of the carload, and went to Mihai's home. Because they had to be back to their assigned churches for the weekend activities, they couldn't stay the night, and it was a six-hour drive back to school. Arpad decided to call his own home from there, and when he did, he learned that his four-year-old niece had died of complications she had had since birth.

"I'll be right there," Arpad said. He called to the seminary, leaving only a message that he wouldn't be there for his responsibilities that Sabbath, and then he left for the funeral in Tirgu Mures. He returned to the campus late Sunday night. On Monday morning, Elder Popa called him in to report about his absence.

"You know you're not supposed to leave without permission," the president said. "Your family called here on Friday to tell you that your niece had passed away, but we couldn't find you anywhere. You did not originally leave to go to the funeral. Let's go outside." Arpad knew that Elder Popa's office was bugged.

"Tell me what's really going on," Elder Popa asked. Arpad had to confess. He didn't want to lie to his director.

"I took a load of literature up to Bacau," Arpad said.

"A 'load' of literature?" Elder Popa's eyebrows shot straight up. He groaned. "Arpad, what have you gotten into?"

Arpad told the president everything.

"I appreciate what you are doing so much," Elder Popa said after Arpad told him. Both of them shed some tears. "I knew it all along. I didn't want to know though." Arpad knew that he could easily be expelled for this. It was hard to educate pastors and then allow them to take risks that could put them in jail where they wouldn't be useful. Arpad wondered if he would be sent home again. Instead he was required to write several long papers as serious punishment, but he was allowed to stay and finish his studies. "We hope this doesn't happen again," Elder Popa said. "I don't want to lose you to prison."

IN HIS HANDS

In spite of this warning, Arpad took his chances. He continued leading the smuggling work for the remainder of his time at the seminary, for it was now in his blood.

Once, he was carrying a bag of expensive books, so heavy that it was hard to carry, when he noticed that somebody was following him. The man in the fur hat looked away every time Arpad looked at him, avoiding eye contact. Arpad crossed the street, ducked down an alley, and into another street. The man was still there, following. Arpad turned sharply and ducked into the entrance of a fifteen-story apartment complex. As he turned the corner, he dropped the heavy bag under a bottom step in the stairwell and bolted to the opposite side of the building, ran out another door and then ran to another apartment entrance beside it. He ran up and down floors, until he found a corner of yet another apartment in which to hide for a while. As soon as he was safe, he called Jakab to go pick up the bag. Less than half an hour from the time he left it, his friend came and found it gone. *Only the government would dare to haul away that heavy, illegal bag,* Arpad thought. *No one else would claim it.*

Another time, Arpad was riding a moped with a box of fifty books strapped in a box on the back. While crossing an intersection, he crashed into a car that had pulled out in front of him. Half of his books spilled out. His elbows and knees bloodied, Arpad knew he was hurt badly, but he had to do something about the books fast. Passersby were picking up the books and returning them to him. "Take it, take it," he told them, refusing to receive them back. "Keep it."

The traffic police came. "Are you OK?" they asked.

"Fine, fine," Arpad insisted. He scooped up all his stuff and pushed his bike to the side of the intersection. Traffic cops weren't as concerned about these kinds of books as the security forces were, but their eyes were always open because of their training. He had lost half of his books but again had avoided capture.

Hungry People

Food was scarce at that time, and all Romanian citizens were given food coupons. One household could buy only two pounds of sugar a month or two pounds of flour. It was illegal to store food in the home. The militia would come and search people's homes, and if people had more food than had been rationed out to them, they would either get fined or sent to jail, depending on how much food they had. Since supplies would run down in some villages, sometimes people went to other towns to buy sugar, flour, or oil. The police always eyed anything that was heavy. Guards at the train station looked especially at large suitcases going onto the train. Arpad was taking a heavy suitcase of literature on the train, but he needed two people to lift it on.

"What are you carrying there?" the guard asked. Arpad knew that even if he said "illegal religious literature" the guard wouldn't believe him. He would have to open the suitcase.

"Look," Arpad said. "I'll give you $50 if you let us go. We have so many hungry people in this village that we are trying to feed. Please let us go." *Spiritual food,* Arpad thought but did not tell him.

"Where is the money?" the guard said, looking around. Fifty dollars was a huge amount of money in Romania. Arpad slipped the folded bills to him, and the guard slipped the money into his pocket. Then he helped Arpad lift the suitcase onto the train.

Not everyone was so lucky. Government agents would search people's homes, and if they found any book printed before 1949, they would confiscate it. Many times church members would pay 100 dollars for a book, the equivalent of a year's salary, and then two weeks later there would be a search and it would be taken.

Then two people from Arpad's chain were caught. They had been trained not to lead the interrogators to the exact source and rather than give out the information of the source, they decided to go to jail. Since the government could tell they weren't the origin of the smuggling, one was sentenced to two years of prison, the other got three. Arpad knew that if he got caught there would be a lot of charges against him. He would receive up to a twenty-five year sentence.

After a few years in seminary, Arpad married Ildiko, his high-school sweetheart. Later, after he graduated he was given five little churches in Romanian villages to pastor. He and his wife had two sons. For four more years he continued leading the ring of smugglers.

But he didn't let the illegal activities stop with books.

The Message

The Trabant, a small East German car, sputtered and choked and fizzled out of energy right in the middle of the road. "We're out of gas," Arpad groaned to the visiting pastor. "And we had only eleven miles to go." Gas was rare in Romania, and the city of Cluj-Napoca, from which they had started that afternoon, had been completely out of gas, but they had to risk the 70-mile drive. The visiting pastor from the conference was scheduled to officiate at a joint evangelistic meeting and Communion service at one of Arpad's churches in Simleul* Silvaniei.

"Oh, no!" the pastor exclaimed. "We have to make it in time for the Communion service this evening. What shall we do? I don't see any houses around here." He looked out the rolled-down window at the cropland around them. "Should we try to flag down a ride?"

"I guess that's the only way we can get there," Arpad said, sighing. The hot afternoon sun shimmered off the worn road

---

* Pronounced Shimlewool.

in front of them. "Let's push the car to the side and wait for someone to come."

A few cars sped by them during the next hour and a half, but though Arpad stood in front of them and waved, they didn't slow down. He had to jump out of the way each time. "Shall we walk?" he asked the pastor finally. "We can't walk eleven miles in the time we need to, but maybe we can find a house somewhere over the next hill. We can see if we can buy gas from them." Arpad took a plastic jug from the car, and they started walking. While they walked, Arpad pondered their predicament.

The Communist government forbade evangelistic meetings, proselytizing, baptism, constructing churches, and children's meetings—anything designed to further the growth of a church, regardless of the religion. Because these activities were prohibited, their value escalated in the sight of the church. In spite of the suppression, Christianity was flourishing. Church members risked their freedom to invite acquaintances to evangelistic meetings. There was always the chance that someone would report suspicious church activities to the government in exchange for an extra gallon of milk a month. Some of the informants were church members themselves. People could trust only those they knew well. Communion, usually held once every thirteen weeks, was a special service of foot washing, grape juice, and unleavened bread, commemorating the Last Supper—Jesus' example of humility and His ultimate sacrifice. In Romania, this sacred service was such a privileged and meaningful time that most Adventists would miss this only on their deathbeds. *All those people will be waiting,* Arpad thought. *We can't let them down.*

At the top of a small rise they saw a farmhouse about a half-mile away. When they reached the house, they walked up the porch steps and knocked on the door. An old man opened the door, very suspicious. "What do you want?" he asked.

"Will you help us?" Arpad asked. "Our car ran out of gas about a mile back, and we are desperate to make it to the next

The Message

town, Simleul Silvaniei. Do you have any gas we can buy, even a little bit?"

The man shook his head. "No. I don't have any," he said. He looked at the sweating men. "But there is plenty of water in our well. Take some."

"Thank you," Arpad said. The man shut the door.

"Well, I am thirsty," the pastor said, "but water's not going to help us get there."

Arpad and the pastor went around the house to the backyard where the well stood. They lowered the cable and pulled up a brimming bucket. They each took a drink, and Arpad poured two liters of water into his jug.

"What are you going to do with that?" the pastor asked.

"I don't know," Arpad replied. "Maybe I'll pour it in the tank."

"What? And ruin the car?" the pastor exclaimed. "That's ridiculous." They started the long mile back. "Water's not going to work, Arpad. It will ruin the engine. Don't you know anything? We'll have to wait for another car. Someone will have to stop eventually."

Arpad raised his eyebrows. "Out here? Now that it's closer to dusk, I don't think anyone will stop now, especially since they didn't earlier." When they reached the car, Arpad unscrewed the gas cap. "Please, Lord," he prayed, "provide a way for us to get there." He took the jug and slowly poured the two liters into the fuel tank.

"That's so stupid, Arpad," the pastor said. "Now we're really in trouble."

"Let's get in the car," Arpad said. He jumped in and turned the key. The engine turned, and it started up without a fuss. The pastor was silent, and his eyes widened in amazement.

"Let's go," Arpad said, smiling. "The Lord is with us." They made it the remaining eleven miles on water, just in time for the service. On Monday, Arpad had the car towed to the shop to have it fixed. The water should have damaged it.

IN HIS HANDS

"It's sure strange," the mechanic told Arpad, "but the water didn't ruin the engine at all. You're lucky." Arpad praised the Lord.

In all his travels to the surrounding churches, Arpad noticed a need for children's Sabbath School materials. Children must stay with their parents through every meeting, the government rule insisted, but still the churches found a way to sneak a Sabbath School class just for the little ones. *The children need color pictures,* Arpad thought. *It's hard for them to visualize the Bible stories, and pictures would help. How can we get some?* Printing Bible story pictures was also illegal, as were almost all of Arpad's schemes.

He had made friends with the diplomats at the American embassy in Bucharest. Arpad soon trusted this Adventist couple and told them about his smuggling and the need for Bible story material to teach the children. They were so supportive that they supplied him with a set of *The Bible Story* books by Arthur Maxwell and also a book with colored prints on Ellen White's life: portraits, birthplace, visions, prophecies, and diagrams of prophetic time. Arpad photographed the vivid pictures, mounted them in handmade plastic frames, and sold them to the churches.

Setting up this business was equally risky. Arpad had a fake passport developed so that he could travel to East Germany to buy the photographic equipment. Except for trips to other Communist countries every two years, the Romanian government forbade citizens to travel. When people applied for a passport, they gave the passport agency their identification cards, and when the travelers returned, they exchanged their passport for their Romanian I.D. card. But Arpad had found a way around this with a fake passport.

Because he had a system with which he could make four times as many prints as the other underground developers made, Arpad sold the prints more cheaply than his competitors and learned to be efficient in the developing process. With this money he earned from selling slides, he bought a car, a

The Message

white Dacia, that would help him travel from church to church.

The church buildings in Arpad's district were old and falling apart. Because the government would not give permission for fixing the buildings or constructing new churches, the conference couldn't give the church any money for repairs. Arpad had to find creative ways to get the job done. Once he worked with his members in one village to build a large family home. When the house was finished, the members tore down the specially designed walls inside to make room for a large church.

In another village, a small church made out of clay was breaking into pieces. Each Sabbath the roof crumbled more and more and in some places it was caving in. Obviously it was no longer safe. Arpad orchestrated a plan, sending his church members out at night to dig a wide trench around the building and pour a cement foundation around the dying church. Before morning they covered it back up again, leaving no trace that there had been any work done. A few days later the workers returned at night with their headlamps and lights. The bricks started coming, brought by church members from every direction, by every means. The bricks came by horse carts, cows, oxen, donkeys and horses, pickup trucks and cars, from everywhere the church members had separately bought and stored them. A group of eighty people uncovered the foundation, built the walls, and installed a pre-made roof with the trusses attached. The new church, built quickly without windows, was much larger, swallowing the old one inside it. By sunrise, it was finished.

Someone reported the new building to the government and soon several bulldozers roared up to the site. Arpad wasn't there, but his church members wouldn't give up without a fight.

"Move out of our way," the bulldozer's driver ordered.

The church members didn't answer him, but they moved into a solid ring around the building and refused to budge. *If it goes, we go,* their bodies announced. Although they were exhausted from their all-night labor, they wouldn't leave their work to be destroyed. For three days they made a human barricade around their new church. Finally, the bulldozers left.

The members then went inside and tore the old church out. The very next Sabbath joyful songs poured from the doorway in the church without windows. The building stands to this day. The government did arrest Arpad, however, and beat him severely, but he rejoiced that his members were getting their needs met.

During this time, the literature-smuggling business was going well. The chain of smugglers knew the system, and the delivery of materials was secure. Everything was working smoothly, and there were two connections in the print shops now. The first was still working for the Communist Army print shop; the second was in the print shop inside the Communist Party's headquarters.

Arpad traveled every week to a new church. He preached four sermons every weekend. He always carried extra bread from a bakery to give to those in each church who had little to eat. (Though buying extra food was illegal, Arpad had developed an underground connection with the bakeries in his village.) He spent his Sundays visiting his members, counseling them, and giving them Bible studies. Then he returned to his home on Sunday night.

One Sabbath he was out in a district church, a long distance from home, when a local church member handed him a scrawled message taken through the only phone in the village.

"Arpad, my husband Bela was arrested with the books," it read. "He was forced to turn in your name. I didn't tell your wife." That was all.

And that was all Arpad needed to hear. His mind reeled, his thoughts tumbling faster than he could keep up with them. His friend Bela Blensessy was caught. There were 10,000 of

The Message

those songbooks that he was smuggling, Arpad remembered. It was proven that they had come from Arpad. He shuddered at the abuse he knew his friend must have been receiving. Because Bela had identified Arpad as the ringleader of the smugglers, Bela would be punished with a lighter sentence. He couldn't blame his friend. Bela's wife must have called Arpad's home to find out where he was in order to reach him. *Bless her heart,* Arpad thought. She wouldn't have told his wife because she knew lines were tapped. Arpad remembered when he had come home at an unusual time once and had seen government secret agents break into his home and leave again, with nothing apparently touched. Communists were not supposed to break into homes when the owners were gone, but they made the rules and they always broke them. Arpad had realized that if he were to complain to the government of the break-in, he would be murdered in a car wreck the next day. If people crossed the government, they were often killed "accidentally" in car accidents. His thoughts continued to leap over each other.

I can't go back home or tell my wife. They will be waiting for me. The smuggling years were over. If he didn't escape now, his freedom was over. *I knew this might happen, but I never knew when.* He said goodbye to his church members, jumped in his Dacia, and with only the clothes he had on his body and his fake passport, sped off into the distance.

That night Arpad's wife waited, huddled with her two sons on the sofa. The boys watched her face that was clouded with fear. "Where's Papa?" three-year-old Norbi lisped, confused. Their mother shook her head, trying to hold back tears. "He'll be here soon," she said, believing that the unsuspecting Arpad would soon return. Waiting at her table sat the police.

Arpad never showed up.

The Double Compartment

I'm glad I have my fake passport, Arpad thought as he drove up to the Hungarian border patrol station. *It's so hard to get these that they probably won't suspect me. It's also stamped with visas from all my trips to East Germany for film. That will be another reason for them to not suspect me.* He remembered the time he had been strip-searched. No worries about that now. He had nothing with him but the clothes on his back. Another time his car was completely dismantled by the border police who were looking for dollars or any kind of foreign currency. He had had to put all the parts back together himself before he could go on.

But this time he passed the border patrol without incident.

I have to get my wife out of Romania, Arpad thought worriedly as he drove on. *Now that I have escaped, they will be watching her very closely. She won't be able to apply for a passport in our country. She'll have to apply for a Hungarian tourist's visa in her hometown.* None of the towns had their information on computers, so she wouldn't get caught if she acted

The Double Compartment

quickly. She must get out of Romania right away. *She'll need to leave the boys with her parents,* he thought, his brain working quickly. *Then when she comes across to Hungary, I will meet up with her. From there I will come up with a plan to smuggle her into Austria. We'll ask for political asylum, and the boys will have to be released to us. We'll be together again. And free!*

The thought exhilarated him. When Arpad passed over the Austrian border, he breathed a sigh of relief. He called a friend, Laci, who lived in Austria and with whom he hadn't spoken in years and relayed the plan through him to Ildiko. But how would he get her from Hungary to Austria? The question plagued him. And then he found the perfect solution.

Laci showed him a gray and blue 1969 Volkswagen van. The van was ordinary in every respect, with an engine compartment in the back. *Hey,* Arpad thought, *if I move the seat that sits in front of the engine compartment, and expand the area into a double compartment, a person could squeeze into that spot. If we build the wall carefully, no one will know the difference. That's how I can smuggle my wife to Austria.* The plan struck him as brilliant. He and his friend worked long and hard to construct the little access area in front of the engine. Inside the compartment he wired a light, hooked to a control switch on the dashboard. He could then send messages to her. One flash would mean "Don't move!" Two flashes would mean "Emergency! I'll get you out of there." The ventilator that drew hot air from the engine to the cabin was converted into a fan to supply fresh air to the double compartment. He moved the wall out farther and replaced the seat so it was a little closer to the front seat that it faced. Over the double compartment fit the luggage, and with the nice paint job and skilled work, no one could tell that the van had anything but an ordinary engine compartment in it. Although Arpad knew this was still a huge risk, he couldn't wait to see if it worked. *Of course it will,* he thought. On his way back to Hungary to pick up his wife, he filled the double compartment with religious contraband to take into Hungary. Since Austria was a free nation, there were plenty of books piled up waiting to be smuggled over into the Communist countries by anyone who had the means. Though he was still running from the Communists, Arpad took a load to drop off. It was in his blood, and he couldn't resist. The mission was successful.

When Ildiko arrived in Budapest, the bustling capital of Hungary, he was ready to smuggle her out.

The morning before they left, Arpad bought a newspaper. He opened the paper and instantly froze. There, on the front, a huge picture spread across the black-and-white page—it was a Volkswagen van. It looked exactly like his own. The headline said, "Man Arrested for Smuggling in Double-Compartment Van." Arpad's hands shook.

"Ildiko, look at this," he cried, "look at this!"

"You've got to be kidding," she gasped. "That could be us. What are we going to do?" Fear descended on both of them.

"We'll have to change our plan," Arpad stammered. "I had no idea this was a popular idea. I won't be able to smuggle you into Austria the way we planned. That will be way too risky."

"Then what'll we do?" she asked, worry large and restless in her eyes.

Arpad thought hard for a moment. "Switch to Plan B."

"Plan B? What's that?"

"We'll get you a fake visa, and you'll fly to Belgrade, Yugoslavia," Arpad said. "I'll have my pastor friend, Sandor Szalma, from nearby Novi-Sad pick you up from the airport. I'll cross to Yugoslavia and meet you there, then smuggle you into Austria."

"But, Arpad," Ildiko said, "isn't there another way? Do I have to get a fake visa? What if they catch me?"

The Double Compartment

"This is our best choice right now. We'll have to go with it."

"Oh," wailed Ildiko. "I'm so scared."

"Everything is going to be fine," Arpad reassured her. "Really!" He hugged her.

Although he could see Ildiko was terrified, Arpad admired his wife for the courage she was showing. She swallowed her fear and agreed to go along with his plan so they wouldn't have to be separated. *I hope I don't let her down,* Arpad thought, *but I can't think of another way.* He called some old acquaintances in the town who had connections and bought a fake visa. Then he called his friend in Novi-Sad, and finally bought his wife a ticket to Belgrade.

At the airport, they watched the plane come in. She gripped his hand. "Are you sure this will work? What if I never see you again?" she whispered. "What if they catch you? What will I do if they catch me? I'm so scared."

"They won't," Arpad assured her. "Your visa looks authentic. Trust me. Everything will be fine." They went to the ticket counter, and everything did go well. They walked to the gate together and waited for the boarding call.

Arpad hugged his wife goodbye. "I'll see you in Belgrade," he said, smiling. "It won't be long. Soon we'll be free." She smiled, brushing away a tear, and waved. Then she turned and boarded the shuttle bus to the plane, her head held high. With the ache in his throat that he always got when he parted from his wife, Arpad climbed to the observation deck on the upper floor and watched the bus grow smaller. He waited till the plane taxied down the airstrip and flew off, a disappearing speck above the trees. His wife's plane would reach Belgrade in one hour.

Arpad left the airport in his van and started driving toward Belgrade. A few hours later, he was halfway to his destination, not yet at the border of Yugoslavia. He went to a pay phone and called his friend Sandor, who had agreed to pick up his wife at the airport upon her arrival.

"Did the plane come in on time?" Arpad asked Sandor.

"Yes," his friend replied, sounding worried, "but your wife wasn't on it. She was on the passenger list, but she never boarded the plane. Are you sure she didn't miss her flight?"

"What? I watched her get on the airport bus. I watched the plane take off . . . Oh, no!" The truth hit, punching him hard, sending his emotions reeling.

"I don't think she ever got on that plane," his friend insisted. "You might want to check back at the airport. Maybe they will put her on a different flight."

Arpad pushed the panic down that was rising in his throat. "Thanks for your help, Sandor," he said as he hung up. "I'll let you know what I find out." He paced the sidewalk where he stood and then dialed the airport. "I'm trying to find my wife," Arpad asked politely to the airport personnel. He gave his wife's name and flight information. The airport personnel gave him a number to call—the Hungarian police. Arpad's heart ricocheted in his chest, and his hands shook.

"I'm Arpad Soo, and I'm looking for my wife," Arpad began when he reached the number. "Can you tell me what happened to her? Is she OK?"

"We've been waiting for you to call," the voice said. "Yes, she's OK, she's just sick. She got too sick to get on the plane. You will need to come pick her up."

Dear God, Arpad prayed, realizing exactly what was going on. *What have I done?* She had been arrested with the fake visa in her passport, identified, and now she was bait to catch him. "Let me talk to her," he said. "I have to talk to her."

"I'm sorry. We can't let you do that," the voice continued smoothly. "Where are you now? Give us the address, and we will come get you and bring you to your wife. Then we can get everything taken care of."

The Double Compartment

Arpad gave them a fictitious address, Posta Utca:2, and the name of Nyiregyhaza, a town some distance away. "Can I talk to her for just a second?"

"That's not possible. Can I take a message?"

"Tell my wife I'm sorry," Arpad said, tears coming into his eyes and burning them. "Tell her I'm so sorry." He hung up the phone as guilt rolled over him, crushing him. He smashed his palm into the metal sides of the telephone stand and wept. Iron-gray clouds loomed in the sky to the north. The red tinge from the sun faded in the clouds to the west, leaving the day dead and cold around him. He looked around at the deserted streets and shivered. He felt a crushing weight in his heart. The police would be coming soon to find this phone where they would eventually trace him, and he must be gone. He knew what he had to do.

Plan C

Why would anyone be so crazy as to escape through Czechoslovakia? Arpad thought, studying his map under a dim light. *Their laws are just as strict there as anywhere. So no one would expect me to.* So here was Plan C: He would circle around through the lion's den of Czechoslovakia, a place his Romanian and Hungarian pursuers would never dream of looking. He would somehow escape into Austria or West Germany from there. Only when he was free would he be able to help his wife. He traced a finger on the road leading through Czechoslovakia. *I've never traveled this way before,* he thought. Arpad put his map down and turned the ignition. He would drive for the border, find a safe place to sleep for a few hours, and then cross at first light.

In the early morning, Arpad drove up to the Hungarian border patrol station, showed his passport and visa, was once again waved through with no problems, and crossed the quarter mile stretch of neutral land between the countries. On the Czechoslovakian side, too, he showed his paperwork and visa. A guard gave him the purple passport stamp of approval

Plan C

and waved him through. He started pulling out of the lane, sighing with relief, when a different officer came out of the booth.

"Hold on," he ordered. "Let me check the van."

Arpad gulped and pulled to a stop. *They won't find anything. They won't find anything.* He squeezed his eyes tightly. The officer opened the rear door of the engine and poked around. He was about to close it when he saw that the ventilator hose from the engine to the interior had been slightly tampered with, the paint a little scratched. He peered closer. He slammed the back of the van and walked to the sliding door on the side, opening it. Arpad prayed. The officer saw the seats and the table. Nothing looked unusual, except that there was a lot less room. "Bring me some measuring tape," he ordered another officer standing by. The officer returned with a measuring tape, and they measured the distance. Arpad couldn't stop them. The blood drained from his face.

"Here," one of them grunted. "What's under here?" They started tearing up the carpet, found the door to the double compartment, and surveyed it with a flashlight. They saw the light bulb hooked up, saw the access area designed for a person.

"Out of the van!" the first officer barked. Swarms of guards came from everywhere. When Arpad opened the door, he suddenly found himself gripped by two guards, smashed against the side of the van, handcuffed, the hordes of Czechoslovakian guards around him, shouting, pointing, beating him, asking questions. Questions. Questions.

They jammed him into a yellow Skoda, a small Czechoslovakian car. Two guards, reeking of week-old body odor, scrunched in beside him. Arpad gagged, the smell almost making him faint. An officer drove the car, and the translator, Major Kardos, sat in the passenger seat. The windows were tightly rolled up, and in the back with the two guards, Arpad thought he would throw up or pass out. He took small breaths, trying to keep his mind clear in the stench. It was worse torture than the arrest had been, worse torture than the questions.

Think. Think! Arpad told himself. *Keep your head straight.* They drove to the prison compound in Bratislava, about a half-hour's drive. There was momentary relief from the foul smell when the car door opened, but then the questions began again, continuing when new officers took over. The questions kept coming, always, and he had to answer.

* * *

In the jail, Arpad covered his ears with his hands in mental pain. Here he was, sixteen days later, and the questions had never stopped, the mental torture of the questions had never ended. The doubt they were trying to instill in him began to itch in his mind. How long could he hold out? And above his steady answers of truth came his own questions for himself. *Maybe I am really lying. Maybe I really was smuggling someone out from Czechoslovakia. Maybe I really am losing my mind. Maybe I have been dreaming all my life. Maybe the Communists are right. Maybe I don't have a God.*

Arpad turned over again on the hard bed, but no sleep came.

Darkness

"Get in," the Czechoslovakian guard ordered. Arpad slumped into the musty heat of a van, rough hands shoving him down to the hard metal bench attached to one wall. The guard's unfamiliar face bent forward as he reached across to shut the door. Arpad wondered why he hadn't seen these guards before, but it didn't matter. Nothing did now. The khaki-uniformed arms holding heavy semi-automatic machine guns blocked his last glimpse of late-morning sunshine and the three-story concrete jail where he had been held hostage for sixteen days. The sliding doors slammed and surrounded him in instant darkness. He steadied himself on the iron bars caging the prison van as the engine grumbled to life, jolting him as it pulled out of the barbed-wire compound. As he bumped down the road toward the unknown, Arpad knew he had seen the light of freedom for the last time.

The sick feeling with which he had lived constantly over the last sixteen days had hardened into stone. *What are you supposed to feel when you face life imprisonment? What do you do when there is nothing left?* He would step out of the van into the train station or the airport; he would be handcuffed, and led away, never to see his family or church members again. He knew the extradition process, the delivering of fugitives to their own countries to be dealt with. He had seen fugitives in this situation with his own eyes when he worked near the border selling insurance. He had heard of countless others.

Arpad couldn't pray. Though he was a pastor, he couldn't pray. He clenched his teeth and stared into the darkness.

A half-hour later, the van slowed to a stop. He heard the front doors opening, closing, the tread of many heavy boots on the concrete. The handle twisted on the side door and sudden light gushed into his eyes, again completely blinding him. The rough hands jerked him from his seat and yanked him out onto the road. A warm fall breeze brushed past him, smelling of hot pavement and forest air. Instead of a train station, Arpad saw a large building to the left with huge sirens mounted in a row on its front face. Two armed soldiers stood at attention on either side of an iron door. The van had parked in front of it, in the middle of the road. Fifty yards ahead to the right and left of the road, a fourteen-foot, barbed-wire fence towered, with its fearsome hooks curling over on the inside. A large barrier made of iron machinery and heavy chain barred the road in the middle. A dense forest pressed in on both sides, stretching before and behind Arpad as far as he could see.

Blinking, he saw twelve soldiers in Czechoslovakian uniform at the side of the road, holding wood-handled machine guns pointed straight at him. Horror and confusion seized Arpad. He was at a border crossing. Anyone crossing a border without permission would be shot—executed. He remembered how fugitives and refugees would throw themselves into the Danube River to cross to Yugoslavia. They had been

Darkness

shot down in the river. The Czechoslovakian government must not have wanted to return him, so they would make him cross in order to shoot him legally. So this was the way it would end. And why not? Wouldn't this be better than the crushing consciousness of life imprisonment? Arpad's throat grew tight.

"Go." The two guards shoved him in the back. One gave him another long push. "Walk." He had no choice. Arpad stumbled forward, waiting for darkness to blind him once more. Where was God now?

The Sign

Arpad's eyes blurred as he walked down the road, inching closer to the heavy barrier. Any minute now and the ordeal would be over. He walked and walked, one foot mechanically in front of the other. The border patrol house was now only a few yards away. From the corner of his eye he saw two patrol guards watching him from inside the booth. As he walked up to the iron and chain barrier that blocked the road between the two fences, the gate slowly lifted up, like a train-crossing gate. Arpad kept walking, resisting the urge to run. No one stopped him.

Where am I? he wondered, confused. *What's going on?* He didn't dare look back, nor did he want to. He still felt the guns waiting behind him. *Waiting for what?* The road with the faded yellow line down the middle stretched another 100 yards before it curved to the right, out of sight in the thick beech forest that grew up to the road. Here and there among the light gray trunks grew the darker trunks of maple and oak trees. Golden leaves gilded the forest, red maples reflected the light, and patches of sun flirted with the shadowy undergrowth.

The Sign

Arpad had reached the bend now, and as he turned the corner, all he could hear behind him was the rustle of wind through the trees. Ahead of him up the road, he saw a simple metal sign painted blue. In black, bold letters it read: *Willkommen nach Österreich.*

Welcome to Austria.

Arpad's eyes bulged. He ran to the sign. His numbness unglued and melted into joy. "Oh, my God," he cried, falling to his knees and clutching the metallic symbol of freedom. His tears flowed freely, cleaning out the bitterness that had grimed up inside him during the past two weeks—his lifetime, it seemed. "Thank You! Thank You! Forgive me for doubting You. Forgive me. I was wrong. Forgive me. Thank You!" *How could I have doubted Him?* Arpad knelt there below the sign, nose to the ground for a few minutes, exhausted with relief, filled with praise, and thoroughly ashamed of himself. *They let me go!*

From his time working as an insurance salesman at the Romanian border with Hungary, and from his lifetime of experiences—the people he had known, the news he had read, the stories he had heard—Arpad had heard of nothing like this. No Communist country would let you walk free. It was unheard of. Arpad knew that the Czechs legally couldn't release him to the Hungarians, who also wanted him, and in order to release him to Romania, which did not border Czechoslovakia, they would have had to send him by train. But that wouldn't have been difficult at all. That's what countries did on a normal basis. There was no reason for them to release him into this free country. It was a miracle.

After a while Arpad stood to his feet and kept walking. Though his knees still shook and he hadn't eaten all morning, his adrenaline and joy made him feel as though he could walk forever. A little way down the road he saw the border patrol station on the Austrian side. He walked up to the guard sitting in his booth. Arpad didn't know German, and only a few words of English. But he knew the only words of English he needed to say.

"Political asylum," he said to the guard.

The guard nodded. Arpad stopped thinking and just let everything happen. He knew he was finally safe.

Soon he found himself in a truck driven by another Austrian guard. About forty-five minutes later he was dropped off at a refugee camp.

"Refugee camp" was the term given to a large square building, four stories high. It was a dark yellow compound with large Austrian flags waving in front. *It looks like a huge World War II army base,* Arpad thought. Inside the central building was a spacious, open courtyard, with dormitory-sized rooms all around it. The courtyard was filled with refugees from Poland, Czechoslovakia, East Germany, Romania, and Asia. He was taken to register, filling out volumes of paperwork on who he was, why he wanted political asylum, and to where he wanted to emigrate. An hour before he had thought he was in jail for life, and now, suddenly, Arpad had to decide where he wanted to spend the rest of his life. He had to decide right then, before he could be admitted.

Arpad paused for a moment. *Where do I want to go? What is the country that I can emigrate to the fastest and get my family with me the quickest?* he thought. *I've always been interested in New Zealand. That's the country I know will accept me the fastest. I've always heard good things about it.* He thought of the temperate climate and the green fjords. *It's a Garden of Eden,* he thought. He wrote "New Zealand" on the destination line. That was settled, and he felt good about it. Now all he had to do was stay at this compound for two weeks until the camp checked out his record to verify his identification and history, making sure he wasn't a killer or thug. If accepted as a refugee, he would be given a place to stay until

The Sign

the time came for him to leave for New Zealand. If not, he would be deported to Romania, where, of course, he would be jailed. Arpad felt sure he would be granted refugee status.

The first thing Arpad did was to find a phone. He called his mother-in-law in Romania who was keeping the boys. He found out that his wife had been sent back to Romania and sentenced to jail for three and a half years. Because she was the mother of two minor boys, however, her sentence was suspended. Arpad sighed with relief. All he would need to do now was ask the country to send her and the boys to New Zealand after he received permanent-resident status there, then ask the Romanian authorities to allow his family to be reunited. It would work out well for them after all. They would all be free, together again.

A New Twist

Arpad found that there wasn't much to do in the refugee camp other than talk to people, but he couldn't communicate with most of them because they were from other countries. He was fed two meals a day. Here he faced his next dilemma.

He had been a vegetarian for twelve years, but now he knew he would have to eat meat because there weren't any other options. There could be no vegetarians in there. His biggest concern was trying to eat "clean" meat. Refugees were given either a white card or a yellow card as their food ticket. A white card meant kosher food, given only to Jews and Muslims. Since Arpad was neither of these, he couldn't have one. He talked to the Hungarian woman at the registration desk and explained the situation to her. "I'll see what I can do," she said. He was given the yellow card. The woman didn't ever get back with him, so Arpad picked around the big pieces of pork in the small serving of mashed potatoes and cabbage. He wasn't allowed more servings of the vegetables. He saw pork, pork, and more pork. Arpad wouldn't touch it. For a

A New Twist

week he ate only the meager portions of mashed potato and cabbage, growing weaker and weaker.

"Please, Lord," Arpad prayed over the tasteless cabbage. "Help something to happen to change this situation. I'm starving to death."

Hunger gnawed at Arpad's stomach. It was the end of the week when, right before the next meal, a stranger came up to him before he got into the food line.

"May I see your food card?" he asked.

"Sure," said Arpad without thinking. He pulled it out of his pocket. The man handed him a white card and took Arpad's yellow card without saying a word. The man disappeared into the crowd as quickly as he had appeared.

Arpad shook his head, amazed. *Thank You, Lord*, he prayed. He ate his boiled beef and mashed potatoes gratefully for the remainder of his refugee camp stay.

The refugee camp finished researching Arpad's story and accepted him. When refugees were officially admitted, they were sent to different locations outside of the compound. Pensions, hotels, bed-and-breakfast lodges, and some private homes contracted with the government to give the refugees room and board. Arpad was sent to a large home with six rooms contracted out. Some of the rooms were large enough to hold an entire family. Since it was warm weather, the camp placed Arpad on a small veranda with another roommate. It was a closed deck with tall windows covering the entire length, and during the day, it heated up like a desert. From the deck they could look out onto the red roofs of the white-brick houses around them.

Arpad's new roommate was a short man with receding blond hair and a round face. He smiled a lot, and two silver crowns capping his front teeth gleamed as he spoke.

"Hi, I'm Mihaly,"* he said.

---

* Pronounced Meehai.

IN HIS HANDS

"My name's Arpad. Nice to meet you," Arpad said. "I had a friend in seminary by your name."

"So you're a pastor?" Mihaly said, smiling. "So am I!"

"Really! How great that they put us together. What church are you from?"

"Hungarian Reformed Church. And you?"

"Seventh-day Adventist," Arpad replied. Mihaly raised his eyebrows.

"How long have you been here?" Arpad asked.

"Let's see. It's been more than a year," Mihaly answered.

"That long! Where are you waiting to go to?"

"The United States. I have all my sponsors lined up, and my family back in Romania is ready to go too. We are just waiting to get our visas approved by the American consulate." He sighed. "It's just taking so long. As you can imagine, I am bored and tired of this waiting. But now I have a friendly roommate, so that will make the time go by more quickly." He smiled broadly, his teeth sparkling. "Where are you waiting to go?"

"New Zealand. It would take so long for me to apply for my kids to come to Austria or anywhere else for that matter. New Zealand has the fastest acceptance rate. In my geography classes I remember thinking what a great place it would be to live." Arpad saw a small wooden chessboard on a box in the corner. "I see you're a chess player."

"Yes!" Mihaly brightened. "Do you play?"

"No," Arpad said, "but I've always wanted to learn. I think we'll have plenty of time for you to teach me."

This was the beginning of their stay together. As they were both pastors and had plenty of time to spare, they discussed their doctrinal beliefs daily.

The Sabbath was a big topic at first, for Mihaly, like most other Protestants, couldn't understand why Adventists kept Saturday. "Jesus did away with the commandments, nailing them to the cross. Now we are under grace. Sabbath obser-

A New Twist

vance is Jewish. Christians keep Sunday because of Christ's resurrection."

"But keeping Sunday is not Christian," Arpad said. "It is not following Christ's example. He showed how it should really be kept holy. If you study history, you will see that the ruling church changed the day of worship from Saturday to Sunday. Sunday, the day for pagan worship of the sun, was a joyful feast day, and after a time, the church declared it holy and the true Sabbath obsolete."

"But Jesus' disciples and the early Christian church kept Sunday as sacred," Mihaly argued. "Let me show you from the Bible why the Lord's day really is Sunday."

"If you can show me from the Bible that the day was changed, I'll accept that," Arpad said. "The Bible, and the Bible only, is what we must go on here. There are lots of traditions and religious materials handed down through the years, but if it isn't based completely on the Bible, then we are living in error."

"I agree," Mihaly said. "But you'll find from the Bible that Sunday is now the true day of worship."

Mihaly and Arpad took a trip through the New Testament. There was plenty of time to argue, plenty of time to discuss. Mihaly had been a devoted pastor to his parishioners and his faith was well analyzed and sincere. Arpad knew Mihaly was eager to get to the root of truth. Arpad's theological training was extensive, and his biblical reasoning sound. Mihaly could not refute Arpad's arguments.

"Let's play chess," Arpad learned to say after every daily discussion. Mihaly would then play chess with a vengeance, capture Arpad's rook, slaughter his bishop, steal his knight, and behead his queen, checkmating with glee. This was one area where Arpad couldn't win.

"How can so many people be so wrong?" Mihaly asked another day. "How come I've never been shown this before?"

"I guess the Sabbath isn't popular," Arpad said, "because

it's the one biblical command that seems awkward to keep."

"There is so much to understand about this," Mihaly said. "Why does your church keep it while the rest of the Christian world doesn't?"

"'There have been many groups of people through the ages who have kept the true Sabbath, in spite of persecution. In America during the early 1800s a group of people from many denominations were expecting the return of Jesus in 1844, as they thought the book of Daniel predicted. When Jesus didn't return, these people studied the Bible earnestly, learning what the date really signified. The Advent believers, not yet a separate church, continued studying for themselves and soon accepted the seventh-day Sabbath. It was from this period of re-evaluation of traditional doctrines that the Adventist Church was formed."

"So did your church completely break off with everything traditional Christians believe?" Mihaly asked. "It seems there are so many differences."

"No, we have much in common with other religions too. Adventists share much of the same faith as the rest of the Christian world," Arpad said. "We believe in the Trinity, that Jesus, fully God and fully man, died for us, and that we are saved through His sacrifice alone. It's all about Jesus. We can't earn our way to heaven."

* * *

In Vienna, Arpad found a Romanian group gathering at the Seventh-day Adventist church. Soon Mihaly attended church with Arpad on Saturday. He grew interested in the Adventist beliefs about the Sabbath, the sanctuary, the second coming of Christ, and the afterlife. Arpad and Mihaly took long walks together through fallen leaves, enjoying their friendship and discussions, especially the daily debates.

The Austrian town of Baden, where they were staying, was a tourist attraction, and people visited from everywhere to

A New Twist

sample wine from the old wineries, tour the historic downtown, and hike up the mountain to the ruins of an old castle built nine hundred years before. The castle stood like a faithful sentinel guarding the valley, unaware that its duty was done and that the rest of the world had gone on without it. Arpad and Mihaly would hike up the wooded trail to the fortress, the forests surrounding them ablaze with colorful fury. Sitting on a sturdy ledge, they often swung their feet over the wall, gazing at the picturesque valley below.

"Do you ever wonder what God plans for your life?" Arpad asked on one such afternoon. "Nothing ever turns out the way I think it will." He threw a small rock over the buttress wall and watched it roll and bounce down the steep mountainside.

"I know," Mihaly said. "I certainly never thought I would be still waiting to go to America a year and a half after I applied. I wonder why I have to wait."

"I would never have met you," Arpad said, grinning. "It would have been lonely here without you. And now I'm learning how to play chess. You never know what the Lord has in mind."

Mihaly shook his head, smiling back. "You've sure changed the way I look at things, but I can't wait to go to America," he sighed.

"I know. I can't wait to go to New Zealand," Arpad replied. " I hope I don't have to wait as long as you."

* * *

One afternoon, only three weeks after Arpad had arrived in Austria, he burst onto the veranda. Mihaly was stretched out on his cot reading, the late afternoon sun streaming in through the glass and heating the room like a sauna.

"Come on, Mihaly. Let me show you something," Arpad said. Mihaly got up, holding his newspaper open with a finger. Arpad thumped a stack of papers onto the table and Mihaly looked at them, poking through the first few sheets.

"Yeah, I know all about these papers," said Mihaly. "I know them backwards and forwards. I already did this application for the United States. Did you change your mind? You're not going to New Zealand now? You're going to America?"

"Yes. I changed my mind."

Arpad flipped to the last page. There, in blue ink, was a visa stamp of approval, the stamp that Mihaly had been anticipating and dreaming of for almost a year and a half.

Mihaly turned red. "What? How did you get this? I can't believe it! This is not fair!" He jumped up, his eyes burning in rage. "I've been waiting for more than a year, my family has been waiting, our whole lives have been put on hold, waiting. You waltz in here and after less than three weeks, in one day, come back with a visa to America. This is cruel. It's not fair. It's not fair." His face was livid. "You got approval in a few hours?"

"Actually," Arpad admitted, "it was in less than 15 minutes."

At this Mihaly threw his newspaper down and stamped off, leaving the room to cool off. When he returned, he was still grumbling, but his curiosity consumed him. "How did something this miraculous happen?" he asked Arpad in amazement.

"I can't believe it myself," Arpad said. "And I wasn't even trying to get one." He ducked as Mihaly threw a pillow at him. "Here's what happened."

Half of Heaven

"I took the train this morning to Vienna, like I told you I was going to," Arpad told Mihaly. "I was walking down a street, looking at people, looking in store windows, just trying to pass the time, when I walked in front of the American Embassy with their big red, white, and blue flag out front."

"*You know,* I thought, *I lost contact with that American diplomat I knew in Bucharest.* The Czechoslovakians had taken all my paperwork," he explained to Mihaly. "So I said to myself, 'Maybe I'll go in there and ask if they have an American phone book so I can look up his name.' I knew that he left Romania with his wife two years ago, in 1982, and that they were from West Virginia. 'I'm going to find his name and call him up. I have plenty of free time, and I'd like to talk to him.' So I went into the courtyard and up to the Marine in a blue uniform standing at the front booth. In my broken English I tried to communicate with him about a phone book and why I wanted one. He left me for a moment and called for assistance. A large woman, professionally dressed, came out from an office. She asked me why I wanted a phone number. Again

I told her, having a difficult time, why I was there and why I wanted it. I studied English in the seminary, but I have no practice speaking it." Mihaly nodded in understanding.

"Now she disappeared inside the offices again and came back with her supervisor, another lady. She spoke to me in a deep voice, and I had trouble understanding her English. 'Please repeat,' I had to ask her several times. Again I told my story, very terribly. She listened, then asked me to wait. She returned shortly with a man, her supervisor.

" 'The general consul would be interested in talking with you. Would you like to talk to him?' the man said.

" 'Sure. If I can get the phone number I will talk to anybody,' I said. I don't think he understood that, but since I nodded my head, he motioned for me to follow him. I went into the long corridor to a very nice office. You should have seen it! A plush burgundy rug carpeted the hardwood floor. In the middle stood a huge desk with an American flag to the right. The man showed me to a leather armchair, and I sat down, sinking into the softness. Then I looked up at the general consul. The man I had followed brought in a Hungarian interpreter, so I could tell my complete story. For the fourth time within minutes I explained who I am and how I ended up here in Austria and that I was waiting to go to New Zealand. I explained I only wanted a phone book so I could call my friend in West Virginia since I knew him very well." Arpad paused, reluctant to make his friend feel bad.

"Go on," Mihaly muttered, still holding a grudge.

"When he heard my story, he asked me, 'Do you want to go to the United States? If you want to go to the United States I will give you a visa today.' My mouth dropped open. *Do I want to go to America?* I hadn't even considered it because it would be too difficult to get my visa and to get my family to join me. Talk about making a quick decision. I thought of you waiting for a year and a half, but he didn't give me any time to ponder. When somebody offers you something like this, it isn't polite to refuse or to ask time to think. You don't say, 'Well, I'm sorry, let me think about it.' "

Mihaly shook his head, snorting. "No, I guess not."

" 'But I'm not registered for it,' I told him.

" 'We'll help you with all that,' he said. 'If you want to go, we'll help you do it.'

" 'Yes,' I said. My heart was pounding, but I didn't show any emotion. I left his office to go wait at a bench in the waiting room by the front desk. I felt numb in my legs. While I waited for the paperwork, I felt broken up inside. I started praying, and I couldn't help but cry a little, in shock. The Lord was working, and it was so evident to me. I couldn't deny it."

Mihaly nodded. "I can't deny it either. He truly did work a miracle for you."

"So the lady came out," Arpad continued. "She gave me a huge pile of paperwork and applications, health documents, medical papers. Then she sent me over to the medical clinic nearby for an exam. I took a bus to the clinic, handed them a special letter, and they took me right in without having to wait in line. After I did that, I stopped at the refugee camp to get help filling out all the English on the application. I wasn't registered for the United States, so I didn't have a sponsor or an organization to go with. They told me that I needed a sponsor in the United States to sign for me and take me in. I still need to find one, but I have a few days. Then I came back here to you." Arpad looked with sympathy at his friend, and his heart went out to him. "I'm sorry, Mihaly."

"I can't believe this happened," Mihaly said, "but it's hard for me to be happy for you. I still think it's awfully unfair." The only thing Arpad could do was to challenge him to a game of chess.

Arpad had to find a sponsor, so he wrote to Gabriel Isaia, a Romanian friend from Bucharest who had immigrated to the United States several years before. Gabriel lived in Loma Linda,

California, and he was willing to sponsor him. Arpad then waited for the World Council of Churches, an organization that helps refugees pay for their plane fare, to find him a ticket. During this time he stayed in touch with his family in Romania by phone and also worked for a Hungarian Jew who owned the Alvorada coffee factory in Vienna. The money he earned there he spent paying for phone cards and care packages for his family.

By now it was deep winter. Up in the freezing Austrian mountains Arpad took a special class required for refugees immigrating to the United States. He learned of the forms he would be required to fill out, the immigration process in New York, language classes that he could take, and other information that would be helpful to his survival. Once while attending the class a band of angry Polish refugees cornered and surrounded him, jealous because one of their teachers had mentioned that Arpad had been waiting to immigrate for only two and a half months. Some of them had been waiting two years. Before he was beaten, friends came by and rescued him.

This time rushed by for Arpad like a dream, a dream in which he was flying, soaring through the clouds. And then one day his dream came true. He flew on TWA from Vienna to Paris to New York. As he looked out of his airplane window at New York curling around the bay as far as he could see, he knew he was in a different world. The zigzag expanse of buildings jutted upward; here and there out of the mass of skyscrapers grew factory chimneys, gray smoke streaming from the stacks into the sky. The traffic moved along arteries through a great body of boxes. The city rose toward him as the plane descended.

Arpad stepped into the terminal, legs aching from his long flight, eyes wide with wonder at the huge airport. After he waited in line, there was a flurry of forms giving him permission to find work, then he got his visa checked and his passport stamped. He declared his possessions at customs and then gave a permanent address.

Huge. Arpad's head spun with the newness, the bigness of the New York airport. Everything was so different—the colorful stores, the expensive waiting rooms, the shiny granite floors, the raised ceilings, the variety of people scuttling by him, talking in many languages.

In an airport restroom, he stared at the toilet. He read the name on the side: "American Standard." There was so much water in the bowl. *If this is the standard for America, I am in great shape now,* he thought, delighted. He walked around the airport, checking it all out—the handles on the doors, little things that he would soon take for granted. *What accomplishments!* He gawked over it all.

He flew on to Loma Linda, California. Emerging from the Ontario airport into the January balm, air so thick and warm for a winter night, the lamppost light shining through the mist on graceful palm trees, Arpad felt he had landed in half of heaven. Moonlight fell on the San Bernardino Mountains, covered with a light blanket of snow. It had been freezing in Europe, and now he was driving past orange groves, planning to visit the ocean the next day, thinking of all the opportunities that this new country held. The life he had left in Romania seemed like the landscape viewed from the airplane window, tiny, irrelevant, and quickly disappearing. His conversations with Mihaly seemed a world away. He jingled the ninety-five cents in his pocket, the only money he owned in the world. What was God's plan for Him now?

THE ARPAD SOO STORY

16

Paradise Lost

Arpad stood on the unfinished roof of the Loma Linda Medical Center offices. It was noon, and he could see the heat waves rising from the pavement on Barton Road.

The dry, hilly countryside around him broiled as he did in the 105-degree heat. He wiped his brow with his hands, browned by the California sun and grimy from his work. He was shaping lead flashing to the contour of a roof drain. In this heat, it felt as though a bomb had gone off in his head, and the smog made his head as hazy as the horizon. "I'm not going to spend another summer here," he vowed to himself, picking up a torch to solder a lead pan for the roof drain. "I'm glad to finally have this plumber's assistant job, but this place is definitely not heaven anymore."

Six months had flown by quickly, and Arpad's original vision of what life would be like in America had been lost in the rejected employment applications. It had been lost in the language he never seemed to fully understand, and lost in the loneliness and inactivity that took the place of his Romanian life. This nation wasn't the land of cowboy and Indian adventures he had seen on the movie screen in Eastern Europe. The Communists had tried to block contemporary Western movies from their people, and for the most part, they had succeeded. But Arpad had seen a few modern movies in spite of this restriction, enough to get a warped picture of American life. In Romania he had dreamed up inventions for practical living, but here in the United States he saw these technological wonders already marketed, available to everyone. The inventions had continually amazed him. But now those inventions were a regular part of life, and he had to have money to afford those things. There wasn't any of that for him.

Though he hated living on someone else's mercy, he had accepted free rent from a kind, elderly couple who lived in nearby San Bernardino. He had applied for a visa for his family to be reunited with him, but since Ildiko had a Romanian prison sentence, he wondered if it would take a year or longer to bring them to the U.S. With phone calls expensive and communication difficult, Arpad noticed his emotional closeness with his family slipping away. He couldn't remember their faces.

The one highlight of his new life was his volunteer position as pastor of a little Hungarian group that met weekly at the Campus Hill church. What an unexpected surprise it had been to discover a band of Hungarians meeting together, a piece of home, in a language he could understand. They welcomed him warmly, and since they didn't have a pastor they soon asked him to be their pastor, an unpaid position. Arpad couldn't dream of a better thing. So this was God's plan for him! With joy he tackled his new responsibilities, even though he barely knew the people. Here was purpose again. He also attended the services of the Romanian group at the Campus Hill church. Another Romanian group was meeting at the University church a short distance away.

This is silly, Arpad thought. *Such small churches should unite and join resources. What a shame they worship separately.* When he was elected to be the pastor of the Romanian group at Campus Hill, he set out to unite the two Romanian groups. He talked to leaders and members of both churches and planned joint social events. He gave both churches attention, mediating their differences and helping members set aside their personal misunderstandings. For the first time in many years, 250 people were worshipping regularly together. He joined a choir that practiced regularly and sang for both the Romanian and English-speaking churches. He rallied the church youth around him, got them actively visiting the elderly, taking trips, planning youth events. To top it all off, the English-speaking Campus Hill pastoral staff gave him an office next to theirs and was very supportive of his ministry, especially since he was meeting the Romanian church's needs better than they had been able to. This position kept Arpad challenged and self-fulfilled.

He finally had found a paying job as a plumber's assistant. He had never dreamed he would be using the plumbing skills he had gained from his two years' leave from the Romanian seminary. And here they paid him $5.65 an hour! Arpad couldn't believe his good luck. Such a fortune was more than he ever had made before. He was learning how to install water distribution systems made out of copper pipes, and his skills grew quickly. Soon he would have a pay raise to $6.00 an hour. The more he could save up to send to his family, the better. They were always on his mind, somewhere, distant, and he knew he must do everything he could to get them out of Romania.

Ildiko. Every time Arpad thought about his wife, he thought of their agonized goodbye at the Hungarian airport. He remembered the relief he had felt when he realized she would be OK. He loved her, of course. But lately he had felt coldness on the phone. Was it him? Was it her? Discouragement filled him. He had heard rumors about himself from his church members, but he pretended not to notice. He wasn't involved with any woman, but people would talk. *If a spouse isn't around, people start assuming things that aren't true. Any little*

Paradise Lost

smile can turn into a tasty bit of gossip. Arpad knew that, but the lonely chill in his heart told him he wasn't going to care.

So he didn't. He had plenty of women around to be friends with, and why shouldn't he? *I won't be unfaithful, so there is no reason to be so reserved and detached,* he reasoned. *Everything will be fine when I see my wife again.*

It wasn't. Arpad's new flirtatious behaviors weakened him. As he felt his character slowly crumbling, he ignored the deterioration, stuffing it into a corner of his busy religious social life. He was a pastor, working for the Lord. Why should anyone question his motives? Yet while he was growing other interests, his commitments to God and to his wife began to grow strangling weeds. Even across the world, his wife couldn't help but notice.

"Do you still want me to come?" she asked.

"Of course," Arpad said. "I can't wait to see you. How big the boys must be now!"

They arrived in February, slightly more than a year since Arpad had first arrived. As they walked into the airport, six-year-old Arpi flew into his arms. Arpad's heart leaped for joy to see and hug his little boys again. Four-year-old Norbi followed, still holding shyly to his mother's hand. Arpad hugged him next, and then his wife. "Hi, Ildiko," he said. "You look great." He smiled at her, willing himself to be happy, to feel what he used to feel, but the emotions he had left abandoned for so long were buried in a pile of recklessness and guilt. This wasn't how it was supposed to be.

After a few months, Arpad asked for a divorce, one of those "American accomplishments" he had never dreamed of. Ildiko agreed.

A deep sadness, thick like the smog, moldered in Arpad's heart. *Why did I allow this decay to happen? How could I have been so stupid? Rather than repairing our relationship, rather than talking about it, rather than taking the necessary steps to deal with it, I decided I would quit. I threw it out because the process seemed too hard. Didn't God bring me through all those smuggling years? Didn't He deliver me from prison? Didn't He send me blessing after blessing? He sent me to America. We were going to be so happy. And did I even depend on Him here to pull us through? No, I went my own way. What a weakling I am, what a shame to my family, a mockery to the ministry, a disgrace to God! What have I done to my kids? My wife? Myself? What I would give to undo this! I was the leader of the home, the pastor. I was the one counseling troubled marriages, guiding couples whose differences seemed too irreconcilable for them to stay together. I am the one who should hold those principles high. And I failed.*

Growing up in a very conservative church in Romania, going to a conservative seminary, Arpad knew that divorce should never be an option. In Romania, church members didn't go to court, but instead took all their problems to the local church board. Arpad had been the church board chairman in Romania and when a divorce occurred like this, the divorcing party would often be disfellowshiped. This didn't happen in America, he discovered, at least not automatically. Should he ask to be disfellowshiped? Wasn't that his duty now that he had disobeyed God?

Before the divorce was final he had moments when he tried to undo the damage he had done. Both he and Ildiko tried. But they just couldn't do it; the will in each of them had disappeared. Now the family destruction was complete, as was Arpad's emotional and spiritual destruction. He couldn't forgive himself. In his charade as a pastor, Arpad couldn't feel God's forgiveness at all. He steeled himself to his fate and waited for something, he didn't know what. *I have abandoned God's plan for my life,* he thought. He felt like Jonah, who had run in the opposite direction from God's plan, only to end up swallowed into the slimy belly of despair. When would the pain end? Would the whale spit him out? Where would he land?

The Journey North

Adela was the dark-haired, twenty-year-old daughter of one of Arpad's Romanian church friends. For a long time she had been just like anyone else to Arpad, but when they started talking more and more, finding common ground, it didn't take long before they were infatuated with each other. As Arpad developed a relationship with Adela, he continued to be crushed by his lost commitment and family and tormented by the magnitude of his mistake.

In the whirlwind of emotions, he felt no real happiness or peace. He had moments of happiness with Adela, but explaining to his children why Daddy couldn't live at home anymore tore him up inside. "I can't forgive myself," he mourned, his conscience a pounding drum in the darkness of his mind. "God, where are You?" he cried. "I can't see Your face. What have I done? Please, forgive me," he prayed. This was a mantra that wouldn't go away. He couldn't feel God's forgiveness because he couldn't forgive himself. *I can't continue pretending to be someone that I'm not,* Arpad concluded. After the divorce, it was hard for Arpad to go to church. Ashamed and broken, like Adam and Eve naked in the Garden, Arpad and Adela ran away from God, as well as from their church and families.

Pastor Villanueva, one of Arpad's friends and a fellow pastor from the church, saw their infatuation with each other and their outward disregard for others' opinions, but underneath this veneer of indifference, he saw their flight from God and from any accusing finger. He arranged to meet with Arpad and Adela one evening in the downtown park in Loma Linda. The air was warm, thick with the scent of flowering spring. He joined them on a park bench under a palm tree, away from the skateboarders and joggers passing by.

"I've missed you, Arpad," said Pastor Villanueva. "I'm worried about you both."

"Pastor Villanueva," Arpad began, "I'm a pastor, but I feel I have given up any right to that title. What do you think the church will do?"

"I can't say one way or the other, Arpad," Pastor Villanueva said. "What do you think, Arpad?"

Arpad took a breath, and then his words tumbled over his tongue as he spoke quickly, afraid he would lose his nerve. "Adela and I feel we should be disfellowshiped. I've tried going back to my wife, but I can't. I just can't forgive myself," Arpad said and his voice cracked. Adela looked down. He looked down, too, as tears smarted in his eyes. When he looked up again, his voice was strong and full, as if he were sharing a long-felt, long-understood resolution. "Please disfellowship me, Pastor. I don't belong in the church anymore."

"Me too, Pastor Villanueva," Adela said quietly. "Arpad and I decided this together." The three were quiet for a while, listening to the unsteady rhythm of cars passing on the road some distance away.

Pastor Villanueva broke the silence. "I know this is truly what you wish," he said, his voice soft. "You are in a lot of pain right now, I can see that, and I am not one to judge you or your decisions. I know you feel alienated from God, and I hurt for you and with you." He put his hand on Arpad's shoulder, and Arpad turned his head away. "Please," Pastor Villanueva said, "don't tune me out. God has not left you. I know you feel pretty hopeless right now, but God will never forsake you."

"That's what I once said to my wife," Arpad whispered, biting his lip. Adela reached for his hand.

"God does not change," the pastor said. "His love is enduring for you, and for you, Adela. There is nothing you can ever do to turn His love away. Arpad, you must keep your eyes on Jesus. I know that this is a critical time for you and Adela. Even though you leave the church, you must keep your eyes on Jesus. He is the One who matters, and He will pull you through. Will you do this for yourself, for Adela, and your boys? For me?"

With a lump in his throat, Arpad nodded. "I'll try," he said. "But He feels so far away."

"I know," Pastor Villanueva said. "But He isn't." Before Pastor Villanueva left, he prayed with Arpad and Adela in the growing dusk, leaving them in Jesus' hands.

After the disfellowshiping, Arpad felt even more alienated from God. To make things easier on his broken family, and to start somewhere new, Arpad packed up what little he had, and with Adela prepared to head north. The elderly couple that Arpad had been staying with had given him an old 1969 Dodge Dart. It was a rusted baby blue, dented and worn out, but working. "It's the color of underwear," Arpad commented, "but it will take us away from this heat." Spring was almost over, and Arpad wanted to keep his promise to himself of not staying through another summer in Loma Linda. Arpad had seen an advertisement for a postal carrier opening in Templeton, about 280 miles away. "Maybe I can try that," he said to Adela. "I'd like to go to Northern California, where it's not too hot."

IN HIS HANDS

Though Arpad was ready to leave, he wasn't ready to separate the boys. Ildiko had agreed that they each would raise one son. "Daddy, Daddy. I want to go with Daddy," said Arpi, running to him. Five-year-old Norbi looked stricken.

"I'll go if my mom goes too," he lisped, hopefully, his dark eyes wide and confused at what was about to happen.

"I'm sorry, but Mom can't go, Norbi," his father said, hugging him.

"Why not?" Norbi couldn't understand.

Adela couldn't bear it. "I won't go," she cried to Arpad privately. "Let me just disappear. I feel like a mean stranger kidnapping her kids. How can I bear this?" Nothing about this departure was easy, but soon the trio, Arpad, Adela, and little Arpi piled into the pale blue Dodge and started up the coast.

A year and a half ago I started life here with ninety-five cents, Arpad reflected. *Now I'm here, thirty-one years old, with fifty dollars in my pocket, and a twenty-year-old girl and a seven-year-old boy. What a combination. I wonder how this is going to work? Things never do end up the way I think they will.*

They traveled up the coast and passed through the little city of San Luis Obispo, where the ocean breeze served as a natural air-conditioner. They drove for another twenty miles across Cuesta grade toward Templeton. When they had climbed the grade to 1,750 feet elevation and started their descent the stifling heat came back. In Templeton they found the same 105-degree heat, but without the smog that plagued Loma Linda. Arpad picked up an application from the post office but discovered the post office took 100 applications, gave a test, and then gave the job to only one person. "It's not worth it," Arpad said, very discouraged. "My English isn't that good. Since it's Friday, let's not stay up here in Templeton. It's too hot. Why don't we go back to that nice little town with the narrow downtown streets? Those European-styled storefronts reminded me of home." By this time in their trip, they had only enough money for one night at Motel 6: $19.95.

The Journey North

Saturday morning crept in through the blinds of their little room. Arpad woke up with an ache in his heart. It was Sabbath. It had been several months since he had left the church, but he couldn't put away his conviction that this was God's day. Maybe he would feel right again if he went to church. He missed worship, the songs, the people, and the peace. Tears came to his eyes. "God, I cannot do this. I need to be back with You. I know I left the church, but I want to be back with You. I want to worship you in church again."

Arpad leafed through the phone book until he found a Seventh-day Adventist church on the corner of Osos and Pacific. It was an adventure to find the church, but after a drive around the town they finally found it, an old church in a pocket of trees in the downtown section. It was small and white. The church looked as though it had been built in the late 1800s. They walked in just in time for the church service. Inside the foyer and again inside the sanctuary, Arpad and Adela were greeted warmly by many people. After being in a larger congregation for a while, Arpad had forgotten what it was like to be noticed and welcomed by everyone.

"What are your names? Where did you come from?" the questions began. Arpad squirmed, not really wanting to reveal his past. "Are you married?" Arpad and Adela blinked at each other. They weren't prepared to answer this one. *How can I tell them the truth that we're not married yet since the divorce is barely over? They might judge us.* He looked at Adela. "Yes," he lied quickly. With this lie he felt he was on a mudslide, clutching for support but not finding any, slipping even further downhill.

One church family, the Wiswells, invited them over for Sabbath lunch. Starving, Arpad and Adela gladly accepted.

After dinner, the Wiswells invited them to a church campout and supper picnic at Montana de Oro State Park. Arpad couldn't remember being among such friendly people for a long time. With their stomachs full of food, Arpad and

IN HIS HANDS

Adela said their goodbyes, not telling anyone they were leaving to find a place to sleep in their car. They had no more money.

"Wait! It was so nice to meet you." Geneva, the lunch hostess, hurried over to shake their hands. When Arpad removed his hand from hers, he was holding thirty dollars.

"Thank you," he said gratefully. *Enough for another night, plus some for food!* Arpad's heart was lighter. *God still loves me,* he thought. *He still provides.* Even though Arpad still hated himself, especially now for lying, he felt a glow inside, a spark of encouragement, the strength to start over.

"Adela," he said the next morning, "maybe this is the place for us to stay. Let's try it." Though it was summer, the cool ocean breeze refreshed them.

"OK," she agreed. "Let's look for work."

They drove to nearby Pismo Beach and found a stretch with motels lining the street. Within a half-hour, they each had found work, Arpad as a maintenance man at Edgewater Motel, the first motel he walked into, Adela as a maid at the motel next door, the Shore Cliff Inn. Arpad knew what it was like to hunt for a job for six months, so this instant find again gave him hope that God was watching out for him. He would make $4.00 an hour, and Adela $3.25.

"When can you start?" the manager asked. "Can you work Sundays?"

"Yes, but not Saturdays," Arpad said. "I'll start right now." The manager agreed, as he hadn't been able to find someone willing to work on Sunday.

Back at Motel 6, Arpad approached the manager. "We need a place to stay," Arpad said. "We found work and will pay you at the end of the week. Can we stay here until then?"

The manager frowned. "No. I can't allow that."

"Look," Arpad said, desperate. "We have this kid here, and we will have to stay in a car in the parking lot."

The Journey North

"That's OK with me," the manager said. "But the cops will chase you away. Let me call the manager where you said you are working and see what I can do." Arpad held his breath, praying, and when the manager finally returned, he handed Arpad a room key. "OK," the manager said, "You can pay me at the end of the week."

Arpad smiled. He, Adela, and Arpi stayed in the little motel room for two weeks, working hard, saving up money slowly and living on bread, milk, and cereal. Together they saved $350 to rent the smallest duplex in Grover City, a nearby town. The bedroom was so tiny that they had to walk sideways to get around the bed. Arpi slept on the floor in the front room. Each Sabbath they attended church.

It wasn't easy going to church because of the guilt that Arpad and Adela felt for telling the members that they were married. But they were too ashamed to tell them the truth, especially now that the church had adopted them. Church members came and brought them a couch, a table, and chairs. Arpi now had a sofa to sleep on in the front room. Thelma, a member who had lost her older daughter, brought over all her daughter's old pots and pans. Arpad and Adela received pillows, sheets, blankets, and a nightstand from various people. With such an outpouring of love from the church Arpad's guilt continued to grow.

"How can we live pretending we are married after all the people here have treated us so nicely?" he asked Adela.

"Maybe we should talk to the pastor about it," she suggested. "Let's call and invite him over. He will know how we should go about making things right." The pastor and his wife came over, and Arpad and Adela sat down to talk with them.

"You're not what?" the pastor exclaimed.

"I can't believe it," the pastor's wife said. "You should be so ashamed of yourselves! Why are you even coming to church? How can you call yourself Christians when you're acting like this? Why, you are living in sin! Do you know what the Bible says about this? What a bad example you are to your child and to the church. They have done so much for you and look at you."

"What we did was wrong, I know," Arpad said. "It was so wrong!"

"You need to go back to your wife, Arpad," the pastor's wife continued. Arpad and Adela sunk lower into their couch, feeling fragile, embarrassed, and afraid. *We deserve this,* Arpad thought. *We deserve it all.* Her words pushed him back. *We want help!* he screamed inside, but her words cut through him like a sharp blade, opening old doubts. *I wish we could get more assurance of God's love. We need support and encouragement. I almost wish we had never said anything. Maybe I don't want to be a part of this church if they can't give us the forgiveness and acceptance we need.*

Arpad looked at Adela, who seemed to be wilting, melting into herself. *Maybe all the members will treat us this same way when they really know who we are. Maybe we should never go back again.*

Resurrection

Deciding to go back to church after the pastor's wife's treatment of them was like going back to the dentist for a root canal. But Arpad knew he wanted to be right with God, even if it hurt. *Why does it have to be so difficult?* he thought. Arpad waited for the pastor to denounce them from the pulpit as they thought he would, but the pastor kept silent about their confession. Arpad and Adela revealed their secret to only a few trusted friends. Slowly, slowly, Arpad regained some spiritual strength. Arpad and Adela were married at a justice of the peace and held their own private and sacred ceremony, committing to follow God together and promising to never let their marriage take second place. Soon the church members began encouraging them to become members. When Arpad had stored up enough courage, again he approached the pastor.

"Adela and I would like to be rebaptized," Arpad told him.

"Since you were disfellowshiped in Loma Linda, I think you should be taken back as members in Loma Linda," the pastor said, his dark eyebrows knitting together as he refused Arpad's request.

It had been two years since the divorce and the disfellowshipping. Arpad tried to contact a pastor in Loma Linda, but his messages were never returned. He finally drove down in person and made an appointment.

"Pastor Vanderburg," Arpad said, "I've tried to get in touch with you to resolve this membership situation. But I didn't get a response."

The pastor nodded. "I know," he said. "I wanted to know if you were serious enough to make an extra effort to communicate."

"I'm very serious. That's why I'm here. How can I be assured of God's forgiveness?"

The pastor smiled. "Have you asked God to forgive you?"

"Yes, but I just never seem to feel it. I haven't found the peace yet. What do I need to do to make it right? Where do I begin setting my life straight with people? I want so much to make things right and be a part of God's family again. I feel so alone."

"Sometimes we need to make things right with the people we have wronged first," suggested the pastor. "You may need to ask for people's forgiveness. Is there anyone you can think of who needs to forgive you? Anyone who you need to apologize to?"

Arpad nodded, thinking of the little church in San Luis Obispo, the Romanian church in Loma Linda, his former churches overseas. "You should also get rebaptized as a sign of your renewed commitment to God."

"I know," said Arpad. "That's my greatest desire."

Arpad wrote a letter to the church board in Loma Linda, asking for their forgiveness. He wrote to the Romanian church that he had pastored, asking for their forgiveness as well. Arpad was desperate to make everything right with everyone that he could. He made an appointment with Ildiko and her new husband, again apologizing for any harm and asking for forgiveness. In order to make things less painful, Arpad and

Resurrection

Ildiko agreed to work together for the benefit of their children. Arpad wrote to the union president in Romania, Elder Popa, who had been his mentor, teacher, and friend. He asked forgiveness from all his former churches and apologized to several other people he had wronged.

Only Arpad's little church in San Luis Obispo remained. *It's harder to confess to people I see every week,* Arpad thought. "God, show me how to tell them," Arpad prayed. "Give me the strength and the opportunity to ask for their forgiveness."

One Sabbath soon after, the pastor preached an especially powerful sermon, making a call at its close and inviting those with a testimony on their heart to share with the congregation. Goosebumps popped up all over Arpad's body and his heart sprang inside him, surging the conviction. "It's time," he heard the Lord say. "Come on, Arpad, get out of your seat." Arpad's legs pushed him up, almost of their own accord. He didn't know what to do or what to say. The pastor watched Arpad from the pulpit. Silence floated over the congregation. His legs trembling, Arpad slid out of his pew and walked to the floor at the front of the sanctuary. Tears caught in his eyes.

"Friends, I am not who you think I am," he said, looking across the faces. Arpad looked down. "All this time I have been living a lie." The congregation held its breath. No one moved. "I wasn't a new member who came, wanting to join your church. I was a pastor who had left his wife." He looked up again, his voice a bit stronger. "When I came here with Adela, she was not my wife."

Arpad spoke slowly, deliberately forming each word. "Not only was it bad enough that I left my wife and dishonored my pastoral position, my church members, and family, but I came here, and when everyone was so friendly, I responded with a lie." His voice choked, and the tears ambushed him. The congregation grew blurred.

"I'm sorry. You have been so kind to us. Please, please forgive me." He didn't know what to do, and then he felt Adela by his side, tears in her own eyes. He waited for the words of censure, or worse, the silent rebukes. Someone's hand touched his shoulder, then another hand, then another. Wiping away his tears, Arpad realized that half the congregation was crying with him, and not only crying, but getting out of their seats and surrounding them, hugging them, putting their hands on their shoulders, and comforting them. "We love you," they said. "We forgive you. It's OK. God forgives you too." Kneeling with Arpad and Adela, they prayed for them both in front of the church. The pastor joined them, and Arpad knew that the pastor too had forgiven them.

In the center of their warmth, Arpad felt another hand on his shoulder, an invisible one that slipped off his shoulder and into his heart, healing it, soothing, and making him free. For the first time in two years, the misery shrouding Arpad's mind was lifted. Inside him, it felt like a fog bank lifting from the ocean, leaving a blaze of brilliant sunlight shining on the swelling tide. *God has forgiven me! I know it now.*

Arpad had been saved from disease, a dump truck, high school failure, secret agents and capture, prison, and a hungry stomach, but until now he had never felt the saving power of God over himself and his sins. He hadn't known Jesus as his Savior. For the first time in his life Arpad understood the grace he had preached about, the grace that had been virtually forgotten in his zeal to work for God. He had lost his ministry, but he had gained a Friend. Being a pastor, Arpad had known his Bible thoroughly, he could argue with the best theologians why the Sabbath should be kept, why the dead aren't immortal, and why there is no secret rapture, but he didn't have a love relationship with God. He knew his doctrine inside and out, but he never knew a heart-felt conversion, never knew the amazing love that would erase his mistakes and set him free.

This is what I should have told Mihaly, he thought, remembering his long-lost friend in Austria. He had heard that

Resurrection

Mihaly had joined the Seventh-day Adventist Church when he reached America. *This is what we have in common with all true believers: A God who longs for our friendship and does whatever He can to bring us home.*

The next Sabbath, Arpad and Adela were rebaptized. The moment when he and Adela stepped into the water of the baptistry was a greater moment for Arpad than when he knelt before the "Welcome to Austria" sign, free at last. He remembered his first baptism when he had stepped into the tin bathtub. Whenever he was pushed down into the water, an elbow or knee or shoulder would pop out again. Immersion had not been possible at the time, but he knew God had accepted him. As Arpad stood in the waist-deep water, he realized that his spiritual life through the years had been much like that first baptism; he was never completely submerged in Christ, his own self continually trying to pop out and have its own way apart from God. Trying to keep too much back for himself, he had been walking only halfway with the Lord. *My baptism wasn't real,* it occurred to him.

As the pastor now dipped him down, the water rushing completely to cover him, Arpad felt the symbolic death of his whole being. As he came up, water pouring from his robe, his hair, his chin, he felt himself resurrected in Christ. He had given everything this time. Smiling, he watched the waters fold over Adela and the splash of her coming up. They both had tears in their eyes. Though nothing was different outside, never had he felt so free, so clean, so motivated, and so new again. "What do You have for me now, Lord?" he prayed.

THE ARPAD SOO STORY

19

Up the Ladder

When Arpad had peace with God, not only his spiritual life changed and renewed, everything did. He felt a new vigor and motivation in his work. Within a year his $4.00 an hour pay had become $7.00. As the maintenance man he made several improvements to the pool and spa, and he threw his whole heart into doing well the odd jobs of wallpapering, carpentry, remodeling, air conditioning, and plumbing. Another contractor involved in the motel's extensive remodeling project saw Arpad's work and liked it. "Come work for us," he told Arpad. "We'll pay you ten dollars an hour."

Arpad threw himself into his work with enthusiasm. The better pay was nice, but it was the appreciation for his effort that propelled him forward. *The plumbers here are terrible,* Arpad thought when saw the work the plumbers were doing. "Let me help," Arpad said, jumping in to assist them. Soon he was doing their work. His boss hired another plumbing contractor to come in and finish the plumbing remodel. The new contractor saw Arpad's good work and offered Arpad a job for $12 an hour. This was too tempting, so Arpad joined him. His new business, C&C plumbing, was large. Arpad had done plumbing in Romania and had learned how to install copper pipes in his job in Loma Linda, but he had never before done residential plumbing using a blueprint.

"Here's the plan for this new house," said Cort, the contractor, to Arpad one Thursday. "Take Paul, my apprentice, as your helper and go do the rough-in." Arpad gulped. *I have no idea what to do.* Rough-in consists of the installation of plumbing and drain pipes in a building before the concrete slab is poured. It was a fairly difficult procedure, especially for a rookie. Arpad held a residential plumbing plan in his hands for the first time in his life. He stared at the blueprint with the technical symbols and markings that mocked him like some modern hieroglyphics.

Because Paul had been working with the contractor for two years, Arpad realized the apprentice knew far more than Arpad did.

"Here's the plan," Arpad said to Paul. "What do you think is the best approach here? Where do you think we should start?" He acted as though he was doing Paul the honor of figuring it out. Arpad agreed with whatever he suggested, and so the two of them began their work. "Tell me what you think of this," Arpad would say, pretending that he was testing him.

"Well, I think it should be more this way," the assistant said hesitantly.

"Of course," Arpad said. "I see that now." He turned his face away so he wouldn't betray his ignorance completely. The sun had reached the brink of the horizon when they packed their tools and went back to the shop. "We'll finish the job in the morning," Arpad said.

The contractor was unhappy. "You're kidding me! That house should have been finished by now. Well, OK, make sure it's done tomorrow morning."

The next morning Arpad and the apprentice tackled the job again. As noon came and they still weren't finished, the contractor showed up on the site. The boss's eyes widened when he saw Arpad's work.

IN HIS HANDS

"What's going on?" he yelled, swearing at Arpad. He jumped into the trench and started ripping out the plumbing. Cussing up a storm, he yanked out all the piping that Arpad had so painstakingly installed. "Pack up and come to my office," he thundered.

Arpad didn't know what to do. "Lord, help me," he prayed.

A scowl plastered the contractor's face. "Arpad, an ordinary, beginning plumber like you doesn't deserve $12 an hour. I thought you were more qualified, but you obviously have no idea what you are doing. I'm going to let you go."

Arpad shook his head. "No. Please let me fix it!"

"What do you want to fix? There isn't anything to fix." The boss's voice grew shrill. "You don't even know what you're doing."

"Look," Arpad insisted. "On Sunday I will buy the materials again myself. Tell me how you want it done and I'll do it. Give me a chance."

The contractor shook his head. "I'm not interested."

Arpad stood his ground. "I've just started. I need this work. I want to be a plumber. I will do it on my free time with my own money. What do you have to lose? Please, give me a chance."

The contractor finally agreed. Arpad went back to the building site with the contractor's directions and began to see what he had done wrong. He worked by himself from early morning until late at night until he was done. The next morning the contractor accepted Arpad's work. Arpad sighed with relief. There were similar houses to work on, and now Arpad did them right.

The next Friday, the contractor sent him to another house where Arpad was expected to do the rough-in again, but this time it wasn't under slab plumbing. He had to install them on a subfloor where he would hang the pipes from the floor joists. It was a completely different project. Arpad had never done this before either, but he started doing what he thought was right, trying to figure it out with the same apprentice, Paul. The contractor came to the site again, and again he started yelling.

Up the Ladder

"I can't stand this anymore," the boss snapped. "You did it wrong again. Pack up and come to my office."

I'm going to lose my job for sure this time, Arpad thought. "Help me, Lord. Give me another chance."

The contractor stood in his office with his arms folded. "Don't worry, Arpad. I'm not going to fire you this time, but I cannot pay you more than eight dollars an hour. You do just what an apprentice can do. I can't pay you for more than you deserve."

"I'm sorry," said Arpad. "But that won't work. I cannot do it for eight dollars an hour. I have a family. My wife is pregnant. I need this money. Please tell me how you want it fixed. I'll buy the material, and I'll be out there on Sunday to do it for free."

Arpad was amazed that the contractor agreed. "Thanks, Lord. You did it again!" he prayed. All day Sunday he worked, and on Monday morning the contractor liked it. So Arpad stayed, but every morning he was in the shop extra early to load up the trucks with materials, not only his own, but everyone else's. Then in the afternoon he came back, checked out on his time card, and then sharpened the drill bits, something that many of them didn't know how to do. He kept up the trucks, kept up the tools, all on his own time. The contractor couldn't help noticing. In a couple of months, he made Arpad foreman, with five plumbers under him.

Now Arpad was working on a difficult project, the Green Dolphin Homes, nice apartments in Shell Beach that earned more money. When Arpad compared the volume of work he produced with what he earned, he wasn't content.

"Look, don't pay me by the hour anymore," Arpad said to his boss. "Pay me piece work. Tell me how much a project pays and let me do it."

"OK," the contractor replied. Arpad put in longer hours. When the contractor realized how much Arpad was earning, he nullified his agreement.

"I taught you how to do this job and now you are taking all my money," the contractor said.

"I am only taking what you agreed to pay me." Arpad said. In fact, I am not taking even that since you have not paid me yet in full for last month's work. I work from early morning to late at night so I can earn something to improve my family's living situation."

"No," argued the contractor. "I'm not going to pay you piece work anymore, only by the hour."

"I appreciate what you've done for me so far," Arpad said courteously. "You taught me a great deal about plumbing. Even though I like the work, I can't accept your offer. Considering my family's increasing needs, I can't afford an income reduction. You see, I am forced to quit," Arpad said. The contractor stared at him in dismay.

Arpad already had another offer. Three months later, almost two years after he had moved to the area, he was foreman on a large development project in San Luis Obispo, making more money. It was here that Arpad re-evaluated his skills and gained more confidence. After weighing his options, he finished the project and quit, earned his plumber's license, and went into business for himself.

When Arpad learned that there were new business laws to keep up with and that he would have no insurance to take care of himself or his family should he get injured or sick, he was overwhelmed. He was the sole provider for his family.

"Dear Lord," he prayed. "I'm too scared to go through this alone. Two are better than one. I need to find a partner."

"I'll be your Business Partner," the reply came.

"What? Really?" Arpad had never thought of God in this role before. "Please, Lord, bless me with the strength to do this, and I will be faithful to You in all my dealings. I will put in the work and You will bless it. We will share the profits."

Arpad and his Business Partner started CalCoast Plumbing. In a few years it was one of the largest plumbing companies on the Central Coast of California.

As his financial life improved, so did his spiritual life and involvement in the church. He and Adela developed strong friendships there. "The greatest asset of this country is its people," he confided to Adela. "I haven't seen people as nice anywhere as I know here," he said, speaking of the church members. "They are so open, so friendly, and so willing to help when we were in need. And now that we are successful, their appreciation and support is just as valuable. When we have success, our friends and the church members are just as happy as we are, even more so. Their friendships have been so constructive to what we are now."

One Sabbath, more than two years after Arpad had arrived in San Luis Obispo, a group of men gathered next to a piano and started singing for fun. A stranger in a suit and tie walked up to them.

"Your voices blend well!" he said. "You need to keep this up." He had an air of confidence. Arpad and his friends looked at each other.

"Who was he?" Arpad later asked.

"Wayne Hooper," said his friend Warren. "He's visiting some family here this weekend. He's one of the best Adventist composers of quartet music. He composed songs for the well-known Adventist quartet, The King's Heralds, as well as wrote the anthem 'We Have This Hope,' for the General Conference." Encouraged by Hooper's comment, the four friends started a quartet, "For Heaven's Sake." As soon as Arpad began singing with this group, the call that he had felt for the ministry, the sharing, the joy became fulfilled. The quartet traveled from church to church, giving worship service programs. All the group members shared in preaching the gospel. Eventually they sang at camp meetings, in churches across the state, and then in Europe. *What a blessing,* Arpad thought. *I am serving the Lord in a way I had never imagined.*

Gradually, another blessing changed Arpad's heart. In the early years of Arpad's business, when he needed two little screws from the hardware store, it wasn't a problem for him to steal them, and pay for them later, maybe. Communism had imprinted upon him from childhood that everything is common property. As he grew in his spiritual life, he learned to see that everything is God's, and everything is private property. Even one little screw had value. For Arpad, this change of orientation was no small miracle.

Many times, out on the job site, Arpad would say to himself, "Here I am, digging trenches when I should be spreading the good news of salvation. Lord," he prayed, "I still remember how clearly You called me to be a minister. If You have a need for me again, speak so I may hear Your voice, and I will listen. I'm ready now. Speak, and I will follow."

Meanwhile, Arpad's business continued to boom. He accomplished two major remodels on his own house. He had a landscaped swimming pool that looked like a rock garden oasis built in their backyard. Often when the sun came up in the morning, he and Adela would sit on their wooden benches overlooking the rolling hills, thinking about how far they had come, how richly God had blessed them. Their minds went back to the times when they had only milk and cereal to eat and a room for one night. Back then they were dependent on God's care moment by moment for their existence. Financial security down the road had been only a mirage. But now, twelve years later, they were content, satisfied with what they had achieved.

Or were they? Arpad wanted something more.

Something More

It wasn't a very big expense, Arpad thought. Just a Ferrari Testarossa, low slung with a sleek red body, sensuous Maranello yellow leather seats, and a strong purr you could feel in your chest. Not a brand-new car, a 1995 model would do OK. Arpad and Zoli, his twelve-year-old boy, looked through the *duPont REGISTRY*™, a magazine that published custom sports and luxury cars for sale. "Adela, I work hard. I don't want to be old before I own a Ferrari, even if I had one for just a few years. What do you think?" Arpad questioned wistfully.

"As soon as you get rid of those traffic tickets on your record, maybe you can think about it," said Adela. "Your insurance for a Ferrari would be sky high. Take care of your tickets first."

"No problem," Arpad said, turning the page. "What'll it be, Zoli? Show me your favorite one." Arpad made some calls to Texas and Florida, looking for his perfect car. He also kept getting more tickets.

"There goes the Ferrari," he groaned whenever he chalked up a new citation. "But this will be the last time." Adela lifted her eyebrows. "Really!" Arpad insisted. "It won't happen again."

But there were plenty of other things with which traffic tickets did not interfere. He bought the latest laptops, VCRs and DVDs, audio and video editing equipment, and new computers. Arpad came home with box after box.

"What did you buy today?" Adela asked him. "You haven't even opened the box you brought home last week. There are still boxes that you've never even opened. Haven't they been sitting there for a year?"

Arpad nodded. "I know, I know, but I had to have this. It's a Sony™ Glasstron®." He proceeded to tell Adela all its newest features. "See, you put the earphones on and wear these goggles over your eyes and then hook it into a computer monitor or television. What you see will be a huge movie screen with surround sound. It's like you're at the movies."

"When are you going to ever use that?" Adela asked, laughing.

"All the time," Arpad insisted, but the gadget was soon forgotten, still in its box. Arpad had found another toy. The only way to satisfy his urge for having was to buy more and more, enjoying it for two or three weeks, and then forgetting about it, like a child's Christmas present in January. He wanted his own "private property" now.

Growing up in a poverty-stricken country, Arpad's family was the poorest of the poor. From fifth grade on, Arpad had been expected to cover all his own expenses. He had always admired technology. When he was eleven, he had stolen his father's prized moped, forbidden to him because it was his father's only transportation. Arpad had only wanted to take it for a spin, even though he couldn't reach the pedals. The police had brought him back, and though he hadn't been scared of them, he had been scared of his father. Another time, a pastor had visited his dad. This pastor owned a small Trabant, an East German pressed-wood car that put out such smoke that it could be traced for ten miles. The pastor had left the key in the car while he went into the house. Thirteen-year-old Arpad had sneaked into the car and had taken it for a joy ride around the town. Again the police had caught him, and he had faced his father's wrath. But the love of gadgets, inventions, and especially cars was in his blood. Now he didn't have to just admire them anymore; he could afford them, and there was no slowing him down. *I've missed too much in the past and I'm going to make it up now, to both my family and myself,* he thought. God seemed to have a different plan.

The phone rang one afternoon in the late spring. Adela answered it, little dreaming that the call would change their lives forever.

"Hello, this is the Central California Conference of Seventh-day Adventists," the voice began. *Since when does the conference start calling its lay members,* Adela thought. *They probably want some money.* "We were wondering if you would be willing to spend some time with an independent consultant to do a feasibility study."

If the conference is actually asking its members for financial help and trying to involve us, then this is wonderful, she thought. "Yes of course, we'd be glad to spend some time." She set a time for the meeting. *What's a "feasibility study"?* she wondered as she hung up the phone. A few days later the phone rang again. The conference employee wanted to confirm the appointment for the next day.

"Can you explain what a feasibility study is?" Adela asked.

"It's a study to determine the desirability and practicability of adopting a plan or system," the voice explained.

"I see," Adela said, still confused.

"The Seventh-day Adventist conference here in Central California has been working on various projects during the last three years for what we call the 'Capital Campaign.' The independent consultant will explain what these projects are."

Brook Saddler, the independent consultant, met with Arpad and Adela, explaining to them the three major projects in the conference. The first one was the Soquel* project, which involved renovating the camp-meeting site that was badly run down. Arpad and Adela weren't too excited. *So much money for a meeting once a year?* The second one was renovating and developing Wawona, the summer camp in Yosemite National Park.

"We can see the benefit of this," Adela and Arpad admitted. "We've had so many happy memories with our boys up there." The third project was raising ten million dollars for the worthy student endowment fund for Christian education within the conference. Arpad and Adela nodded. "Now this is a worthy cause," they agreed. Arpad and Adela had paid all their children's tuition, even helping to pay tuition for other children who couldn't afford to go to Valley View Adventist School in Arroyo Grande. Christian education was important to them.

"Are you willing and able to support any of these projects?" Brook asked, seriously.

"Yes." Arpad leaned back on his green leather sofa. "We'll probably contribute something."

"How much would you consider giving? Think about it, and talk it over." Brook spoke with weight in his voice. Adela felt as though his eyes were measuring the dimensions of their souls. Brook prayed with them, then stood up and shook hands with them. After he had left, Arpad and Adela sat at their kitchen table.

"How about that? This is great, isn't it, Arpad?" Adela asked. "Remember how many times we have talked about the bad condition Wawona is in, and how we have hoped that the conference would do something about it?"

"Finally, some action. I like it!" Arpad exclaimed. "It's the

---

* Pronounced SoCal.

educational endowment idea that I like the most. That's my dream: to make Christian education affordable for any child who wants it. I'm impressed with the conference taking on such a challenge. It got my attention. How much do you think we should give to this project? Five thousand? Ten thousand?"

"Slow down," Adela said, laughing. "That's a lot of money. Let's pray about it, and give it some more thought."

A short while later, Marie Redwine, the director of the Capital Campaign, called and set up an appointment with Arpad and Adela. Marie, a petite woman in her late thirties, had long brown hair and an energetic smile. The three felt an instant connection and talked with the ease of long-time friends. Marie gave the Soos more information regarding the conference projects, answered some of their questions, and then asked directly, "Would you join the volunteer fundraising team for the Capital Campaign? We need people like you."

Arpad smiled, sending a silent prayer. *Lord, You heard me again. I missed working closely with You. You sent a messenger letting me know you have more work for me.*

"Yes," Adela said, startling Arpad by speaking his thoughts. "We want to get involved with this project. I see it as an answer to our prayers. You know, for a while now we have been asking God to ready our hearts so we could respond positively when He calls us to work in His field." They were sitting outside on a beachfront where they could oversee Adela's niece and nephew building sandcastles. The ocean breeze was gentle. Arpad spoke, nodding his head.

"It's true. We have been so busy building our home and business, and we were afraid our hearts might get too attached to these earthly treasures. So you see, God answered our prayers through this opportunity to focus on eternal values."

Two weeks later, Marie called again and set up a time to visit them again, this time with Jerry Page, the conference president. Arpad and Adela were curious, yet pleased. "Why would the conference president want to visit with us? Since we've been here for thirteen years," Arpad said, "we've never seen a conference president visiting our little church. Because our church is so small, we've felt like the conference leadership was not interested in being involved with us, especially in lay members' lives."

"I know," said Adela. "Whenever we've been in their presence, it didn't seem like they even noticed us. I wonder what he'll be like in person."

Jerry and Marie met with them at their house. Arpad shut off all the phones so he could concentrate. They introduced themselves to Jerry and sat on the comfortable sofas, sipping lemonade. Jerry was a tall, secure man, who was interested in knowing about Arpad and Adela's family and encouraged them in their everyday challenges. "We have three boys," Arpad said quietly. "I know every parent worries about their children, and when we look into the future, it scares us not knowing which direction they will head. I remember how I was before I found Christ. They must make their own decisions."

"It's true," Jerry said. "But no matter what road they take, they are still within reach of the Savior. Whatever happens in their lives, never stop praying for them. God reached me when I was as far away as I could get." Jerry told them about himself and his family. Life hadn't been easy for him growing up. He had struggled as a teenager, rebelled, done drugs, and had gone as far away from God and the church as he could. But God had still found a way to touch his life, and he had turned around, giving his life to serve God. Jerry asked to pray for Arpad and Adela right then, asking God for the blessing that Jerry had received, praying for their boys, that as they grew up God would protect them and give them the strength to come out of whatever darkness would surround them. Arpad and Adela felt peace and closeness with Jerry that they hadn't expected to find in a church leader. In Arpad and Adela's eyes, Jerry became human, a vulnerable man, someone who had walked in the shadows of life but through God's grace had emerged into sunlight.

Their conversation moved to the Capital Campaign. Suddenly Marie smiled and cleared her throat, and direct as always, spoke. "So, do you think you could pledge the Capital Campaign $_____?" She named a very large amount.

Arpad stopped sipping his lemonade. He stared at Marie. "Huh?" He looked at his silenced pager. Already nine messages had come through. Adela covered her mouth and coughed, or was it a laugh? She got up from the sofa, trying to keep a straight face. She noticed Jerry's glass was empty. "Would you like some more lemonade?" she asked him. She walked over to the kitchen to refill his glass. *She must be joking!* Adela thought, and she laughed to herself.

The thought came out of nowhere, but it was so strong that it took Adela by surprise. An image of an old, wrinkled woman, listening to the voices of her husband and their guests outside a tent. Adela saw the biblical Sarah, laughing at the prediction that she, an elderly woman, and her 100-year-old husband, Abraham, would have a son. One of the Guests outside the tent asked Abraham, "Why did Sarah laugh? Is anything too hard for the Lord?"[*]

Adela immediately thought of what had happened a year later: Sarah had had a son. *Probably God is talking to me now, and I'm laughing about it. God has given us so much, and I haven't given much back to Him. I haven't been challenged.*

In the living room, a half-smile curled up Arpad's right cheek. "You're pulling a good one!" he said. "You almost had me fooled." He chuckled, then stopped. Arpad stared at Marie and Jerry, but their faces were straight and serious.

---

[*] Genesis 18:9-15. All Bible texts are from the New International Version, unless otherwise noted.

THE ARPAD SOO STORY

21

Lost and Found

"OK, so they weren't joking," Adela said when Marie and Jerry had left. Arpad and Adela had promised to think and pray about the contribution. "That's a lot of money!" Adela exclaimed. "We don't have that kind of money to throw around." Arpad was thinking of his Ferrari. "Who do they think we are?" Adela continued as she put the lemonade glasses in the dishwasher. "We work hard and want to give back to the Lord, but this isn't a little donation for a mission trip they're asking us to give. We don't have this kind of money. This commitment is more than I am comfortable with. Why, it's ridiculous!"

"Yes," Arpad said, combing his hand through his hair. "I really thought they were joking. They asked for many times more than what we considered giving. Can you believe it? You know, though," Arpad paused, smiling, "the question made me feel rather good." He patted his chest. "They think I can afford this. I feel respected." He looked at his pager lighting up with business calls. He hadn't had time for this meeting, and now Marie and Jerry's visit left him distracted. What really disturbed him was that he felt God touching

Lost and Found

his heart. *Is this really Him?* he wondered, trying to shake off the conviction. "I'm in a rush to get back to the job site," Arpad said, going out the door. "We'll have to talk about this later." *So much money!* Arpad's thoughts were stuck on repeat as he drove toward town. *How much money is that? He tried to calculate it in his head. Aghh. I can't even think how much that is.* He shook his head, trying to clear his mind. The numbers were heavy stones hurled into his calm life, splashing, multiplying into tiny waves that rippled throughout his whole being. *So much money!*

Arpad's thoughts continued to pummel him. *That's asking me to dig out of what I don't have. We just got back from a trip to Europe, and we spent more than I was planning to. I wanted to give Adela a nice trip next year, but we won't be able to afford it now. Our house isn't paid for. We're living on borrowed finances. We have so much debt. Where are we going to come up with that kind of money? There's no way. It cuts too deeply into our life. Why, that's asking me to give up my Ferrari. No! We'd have to sacrifice more than that, and even then, how could we do this?*

"Arpad," the small voice spoke in his mind.

"Huh?" Arpad knew that voice.

"I gave you all you own. Everything you have comes from Me."

"But, Lord," Arpad grumbled. "We started from nothing. We don't have that kind of money. They should be asking someone else," he answered out loud.

"It's not the amount of money that counts," the thought replied. "It's that you are asked to give beyond your comfort zone. I have prepared you, Arpad. This is why you're here. You are ready. It is your turn to give."

Arpad's eyes widened. He hadn't thought of this before. "You always seem to have another plan up Your sleeve, Lord," he said. "I didn't always trust You when things were going bad, am I now going to doubt You when things are going well? If You will provide, then we can do it, even the impossible."

IN HIS HANDS

Tears welled up in his eyes. "Lord, You have done so much for me. My priorities lately have been all wrong."

It was as if a dam broke, and encouragement rushed in, filling him with conviction. "Yes, of course! I want to do this! We need to. There is a housing project that might come through for us. That will be the only way I can think of. This will be hard, but I bet we can do it. I must talk to her right now." He dialed Adela on his cell phone, but the line was busy. *I want to talk to her before I chicken out,* he thought. *Adela, get off the phone.*

After Arpad left, Adela went into the home office and went through their accounts. She couldn't stop thinking about the request.

"Why do I need to think about this?" she said to herself. "Everything I have is a gift from God anyway. Why am I putting this off?" She felt the pang in her heart, two conflicting values at war. "But we started with nothing in our stomachs, scraping to get enough food for our next meal. There's no part of being deprived and poor that we haven't been through, and now God wants us to give up this security?"

Adela added up the numbers: their income, their investments, their savings, the bills, their debt, everything. No matter what angle she picked, even if she stood on her head, the numbers didn't add up to supply the requested donation. *Maybe I'm doing the wrong formula,* she thought.

Well, Adela thought, *we have enough equity in the house to make our pledge. That, and if the new contract for the housing development goes through, we might be able to make it. We'll have to sell the house, scale down, and buy a smaller house. We will have to dip into our retirement savings and our sons' unused college savings, and what we have set aside for "rainy days." We could build some spec homes and dedicate the proceeds of one of them to the Lord. Cutting back on our expenses will be hard.*

"Adela," the voice interrupted softly. "I will provide. I gave you everything—your material possessions, your home, your

Lost and Found

happiness. I even gave you My life. Don't you see? Don't you understand? Is anything too hard for Me? I want to use you and your resources to further My work." It wasn't a command, just a gentle statement.

"Me? Really?" She felt a conviction pick her up and lift her out of her organized, perfectly planned existence. *What an honor,* she thought. *God wants to use me! Yes, our priorities have been all wrong. I must call Marie before she gets back to the conference office so she can have an answer to give them. I have her cell number on her business card.* Adela straightened her back and took a deep breath. "I need to call Arpad first," she said. "How should I tell him? Will he agree with me? Will he give up his Ferrari dream? If it weren't for those tickets he keeps getting, he'd already have one by now. He'll be so disappointed." She dialed Arpad's cell phone several times, but each time she heard the busy signal. "He must be on one of those pager calls. Come on, Arpad, hang up the phone."

She dialed Marie's number before she could lose her motivation. "Wait! I haven't even talked to Arpad. We do all the financial decisions together." Marie's phone was ringing. Adela hung up quickly as her heart pounded. "I can't call her without talking to Arpad. I know him. I know he will agree with me that our priorities have been wrong, but I must consult with him first. I can't talk to Marie yet."

The phone rang. *Maybe it's Arpad,* she thought.

"Hi, this is Marie. Did you just call me?" She had a digital cell phone that had recorded Adela's number. *Oh, no!* Adela grimaced.

"Uh, yes," Adela said. "I called you. I've thought about your request, and it makes sense that I give this money back to God's work to be used in this project." She spoke quickly.

"Uh, Thank you! Wow!" Marie sounded stunned. "I'm speechless. I don't know what to say. Thank you." Marie promised to get back with them. The phone rang again.

"Hello?" Adela answered.

IN HIS HANDS

"Adela," Arpad said on the other line. "I've been trying to get through. Every time I called the line was busy."

"I was trying to call you," Adela said.

"Oh! You know, I've been thinking about this, and the more I put it off, the worse it will be. I've changed my mind, and I think our priorities have been all wrong. I don't want to talk myself out of it. Let's just pledge this money."

Adela smiled. "Good. I already did."

"You what?" Arpad gasped.

"I'm glad you feel that way too because I just told Marie we were going to give them the money."

Arpad's mind clouded over. *Hey, wait. We talk everything over. This is a major commitment. This isn't a dress she bought without consulting with me.* He was silent. Then the conviction returned, stronger. "Adela, there is no question that God was working at the same time in both our hearts. This was no coincidence."

Adela sighed with relief. "I think so too. I didn't mean to tell her without you, but it just happened."

"I understand," Arpad said. "I can't describe the joy I have in my heart right now. It feels better than if someone had offered me a hundred thousand dollars. Finally I can return something substantial to God. We have received so many blessings."

"I know," Adela said. "I know we have been returning our tithe and we have helped with lots of smaller church projects, but every time we've given, it has been from what we had extra. Well, not extra maybe, but it wasn't really out of our comfort zone. This time is different. We are going to have to sit down and make a plan."

Arpad jumped in. "We will have to give up a lot from ourselves in order to make this work. I know it won't be easy, but maybe this is what the Lord had in mind. I guess I understand the term 'planned giving' better. It never made much sense before."

Lost and Found

Arpad's dream Ferrari roared into his thoughts, spun a tight doughnut in the road, gunned its 400-horsepower engine, and squealed off into the distance, vanishing out of sight. *I'll be so much happier to see kids running around in a beautiful summer camp having fun, than to see myself driving that Ferrari, telling kids not to touch it.* The desire to have a Ferrari disappeared, along with Arpad's desire to compete for financial success. Something had changed inside him, and he saw the transformation in Adela too.

That night Arpad and Adela sat down to figure out the finances. It was as tough as they thought it would be, maybe tougher. They split the payments for the pledge into quarters for the next two years.

"We still need to think this through," Adela said. "Do you think we made a rash decision while caught up with emotion? It all happened so fast. What if we don't close the deal on the new contract? What if we are assuming this is God speaking to us? Since the math didn't add up, what if we don't have the resources to back up our pledge?"

"No, I still think we made the right decision," Arpad said. "It feels good to know that we're now working to provide for a greater cause than our own selves. God will provide as He always has. Let's not give Him conditions, but do our part regardless of how hard it will be."

Adela nodded slowly, but she still felt a gnawing of worry inside. They went to bed, and Arpad hadn't slept so well for a long time. The morning sun woke Adela earlier than usual. She went downstairs, as usual, to have her devotions and sip her coffee.

"Arpad! Arpad!" He heard his name called.

What? What's going on? "Is something wrong?" He shuffled out of bed and came down the stairs. "What is it? What happened?"

Adela, wrapped in her red bathrobe, ran to him. "Arpad, look! Look what I found! I found the answer."

Heaven's Floodgates

"Arpad, I was praying that God would reassure me that we have done the right thing," Adela said as Arpad came into the room. "I kept feeling that maybe we had acted out of emotion and maybe even guilt. These second thoughts kept coming to haunt me, even though my heart tells me we did the right thing."

"I know what you mean," Arpad said, sitting down next to his wife. "The decision still staggers me too. But what did you find?"

"I was praying for His voice, and when I flipped open the page on my daily devotional calendar for today, I found this text." Adela pointed to the words. "I've read it a hundred times before, but it says something entirely new to me now." Arpad read:

> "Do not store up for yourselves treasures on earth, where moth and rust destroy, and where thieves break in and steal. But store up for yourselves treasures in heaven, where moth and rust do not destroy, and where

thieves do not break in and steal. For where your treasure is, there your heart will be also" (Matthew 6:19-21).

Arpad's heart fluttered, and he looked at Adela with amazement. Adela opened her Bible and read the verse again.

"This is no coincidence, Adela," Arpad said. "I've lived long enough and seen God's hand in my life so many times that I know better. This is assurance that what we did was according to His plan. He is my Business Partner, after all. How could I have forgotten this?"

Adela nodded. "It is like God telling me directly, 'Your heart and money are now in the right place. You don't have to feel worried or bad about the future.' Arpad, now I have confidence that God is in control. My treasure isn't here, and I'm not going to store it on this earth anymore." Adela brushed a tear from her eye.

Arpad looked through the glass doors to the pool. "I feel guilty for putting so much money into remodeling this house and building our pool and backyard when there is such a great need in God's work. But it's too late to change this now. How can we make this right?"

"Let's pray and ask God to turn it into a blessing," Adela suggested. "Every possible time we can, we will share our home with others. It will always be open for God's work, to anyone who needs a place to gather for meetings or to have fun or a place to stay."

Arpad and Adela hugged each other at the bottom of the stairs and prayed, their hearts filled with the warmth of gratitude, and their outlook changed.

Arpad sensed that other things in his life were changing too. He stopped bringing home boxes of stuff, he stopped looking and lusting over the newest mechanical inventions that he just had to buy, and he stopped wanting to "have." The shift of desires and interests was so dramatic that Arpad could hardly believe it. It wasn't that he had decided he shouldn't buy anymore because of their campaign pledge, though that contributed to it, but it was more than that. The desire to shop and own things was gone completely. As he had as a child, Arpad felt God's healing touch, this time in the polio of materialism, the disease that had crippled and stunted his spiritual life.

Arpad thought about the unusual business opportunity that had turned up the week before. He had received a request to bid on a new job for a project of 180 homes in Santa Maria, the Cherry Blossom development. *Wow! This big project is the answer to our prayer,* Arpad thought. *God is already providing for this commitment we have made. He answered before we prayed.* Arpad talked to the builder and put a good package together for him. The profits from this project would make the payments toward the Capital Campaign pledge easier. He waited for the builder to accept his offer on Monday. Instead, the builder called to turn him down. "We're giving the job to another plumber," the builder told Arpad.

What? How can this be? The news crushed Arpad. "God, were You just trying to tease me? You answer my prayer only to have it fall apart? What's going on?" Arpad couldn't help but sulk. "I guess this isn't Your plan. All right." Discouraged, he went on with his regular business. A couple of days later he went to the plumbing supply house and ran into the plumber who had been given the project. Since Arpad knew who he was, he struck up a conversation, even though he still held a little grudge.

"Hi, Mark, I heard you got the Cherry Blossom project in Santa Maria," Arpad told the man. "Congratulations."

"Thanks," Mark replied. "The Lord is so good. I am so blessed to get this. You know, I was completely out of work and I would have had to lay off all my employees, some of them who belong to my family. I was at such a desperate point, and then the Lord sent this project to me. I am so grateful."

Heaven's Floodgates

Arpad stepped back, his heart feeling as though it had flipped upside down. His conscience smote him. "I'm so happy for you!" he told the man. "Yes, the Lord sure knew what He was doing." *How could I have been so vain?* Arpad reproved himself. *The Lord is wonderful, and He has other children. It's not about me or this Capital Campaign. He sees the whole picture and blesses all who need Him.* Arpad felt peace again. *It's still in His hands.*

Soon Arpad felt those Hands putting another opportunity in his way. A building company from southern California was in the area looking for a plumbing company for a thirty-eight-home project right on the beach in Morro Bay, an expensive area that sold to Silicon Valley buyers who were purchasing weekend homes running $700,000 and up. The company chose Arpad for the plumbing job. "Just name your price and do the job," they told him. *Why, the profit on these thirty-eight homes is greater than that from the 180 homes in Santa Maria,* Arpad thought, stunned. *It's less work for more money.* "God, You had it all planned," Arpad rejoiced. "You had the right job in mind for us, but we just had to wait."

But heaven's floodgates were far from dry. Another job with a substantial return appeared, a subdivision of 100 upscale homes. Arpad's business grew stronger. "Lord, this is all You," Arpad said, even more amazed. "I never dreamed You would bless this much."

A while later, the builder who had turned Arpad down called him back. "Arpad, will you come talk to us? Mark can't keep up, and he's far behind. There are twenty houses standing around without plumbing in them, and that really hurts us financially. Come down and name your price."

"What about Mark?" Arpad asked. "Are you still keeping him on?"

"Yes, he has plenty to do. We just need you to do the work that he can't get to. Will you help us out?"

"Of course," Arpad agreed. "Praise the Lord," he told Adela. "There is more gain in this project than there would have been had we been given it in the beginning. The number I was thinking of was too low for God's vision."

Arpad and Adela built four houses for an investment, and they dedicated one of the houses entirely to the Capital Campaign. That house sold right away, while the other three homes took a while.

Since Arpad and Adela had told Marie that they would be co-chairs of the volunteer fund-raising committee for the Capital Campaign, Marie had asked them to come to the conference constituency meeting at the upcoming camp meeting. The constituency meeting would be composed of delegates from all the conference churches, casting their votes for or against the Capital Campaign fund raising, as it was not official yet. It could be the meeting to kick off the year's fund-raising project.

"Why don't you come for the whole week?" Jerry Page had suggested. "We'll find you an RV spot since you haven't made reservations. The meetings go from Friday morning through the following weekend. Arpad, would you tell your story at the first meeting on Friday morning?"

Adela and Arpad conferred. "We've never been at a camp meeting for the whole week before," Arpad said. "And we have so much work to keep up with. It's a ten-day event. I don't think I can take that much time off."

"Well, it would be nice for me to spend time with Zoli there," Adela reasoned.

"Tell you what," Arpad said, "I will take you and Zoli up to the campground on Thursday, give my testimony on Friday morning, spend Sabbath there, and then drive back here to do business. Then I'll return for the following weekend. It's a three-hour drive. Let's see if we can borrow Gilder's motorhome." Adela agreed.

On Thursday evening near sunset, Arpad, Adela, Zoli, and a friend were heading for Soquel. About halfway to the camp-

Heaven's Floodgates

ground, they reached a long, deserted stretch of road. Green and brown rows of cropland stretched all around them as far as they could see in the growing darkness. Suddenly, the motorhome shuddered and lost power. From the top of a small knoll, Arpad coasted the motorhome down to a country gas station. There were no homes or towns in sight. An attendant with a gray, grease-splotched shirt was still in the garage, though it looked as though he was closing shop. He came over and checked the motorhome's engine.

"Both batteries are completely drained," he said, "and your alternator is shot. Let me see what I have." He disappeared into his shop and returned with tools and an extension cord.

"Sorry," he said. "I do not have a replacement alternator that fits your motorhome. You won't be able to drive on those drained batteries. "You'll have to stay here for the night. Here is a cord. You can hook to that outlet there and get some electricity."

"So much for the Friday-morning testimony," Arpad said. "Oh, well. There's no use worrying about it. We'll try to have a nice time here." He called Jerry Page on his cell phone. "Sorry, Jerry, we are stranded halfway up there, without any power in our motorhome. We probably won't be able to make it for tomorrow morning."

"I understand," Jerry said. "But we'll be praying that you do."

The next morning as soon as it was light, Arpad turned the key in the ignition. The engine roared to life as if nothing had gone wrong. They started down the highway again, driving more than 100 miles on a "dead" battery and arrived at the camp meeting a few minutes before the meeting was to start. Arpad delivered his testimony after all.

"In every step we've made since our commitment to the Lord we've seen miracles," Arpad said. "Maybe they were all around us before, but perhaps we didn't see them because we had a different attitude. Now we see God's hand in everything."

Arpad stayed through the first camp-meeting weekend. He enjoyed the seminars and meetings so much that he didn't want to leave on Saturday night. "Adela, I'm staying here. I want to be a part of this. This is more important than work. I'll just drive home to take care of the quarterly reports and payroll and then drive back."

That day he drove a rental car three and a half hours home and then back, arriving just in time for the evening meetings. He didn't want to miss one. Arpad had never before seen camp meeting as a valuable time. When he had come before, just for Sabbath, he had found it difficult to settle into a spiritual mood. He learned that when he was there he had time for meetings, for his family, and for growing a more trusting relationship with God. With each meeting he soaked in a spiritual blessing.

"Adela, I never knew what a difference coming to camp meeting the whole week would make on me," Arpad said.

"I know," Adela said. "I can't relax with only a three-day weekend. Staying here longer gives me time to submerge into it, and the more I listen and attend the meetings, the more I feel the Holy Spirit working in my life and the more chances I have that I will remember all this when I leave. We've been maxed out on vacations, but this one is different. This is such a good value for our family. The children are safe, and it's exciting to see the young people sharing their faith."

"Let's reserve a space for next year right away!" Arpad said.

"God has his timing," Pastor John Nixon, the evening speaker, preached one evening. "God started answering one of my prayers nine years before I had even prayed it. I couldn't see it at first. I didn't understand what God was doing sometimes, but now I can see how God was working even back then in my darkest times to answer my future request."

Arpad squeezed Adela's hand as she sat beside him. *How true,* he thought. Events in his life were starting to make some sense that he had never seen before. His whole life was a giant puzzle pieced together with mistakes, doubts, and selfishness, fitted together with God's victories, God's deliverance, and God's purposes. Looking back on his early life, he could barely recognize himself. *God used me to smuggle His messages to thousands of people when I lived in Romania, and now He is still using me for furthering His work.*

It's still about risk, the risk to put everything on the line for the Savior, whatever it is that He needs. Arpad felt a feeling of freedom surge within him. He had an expert Guide planning his life. *Without Him I'm as well off as I was in that Czechoslovakian jail. And it's not about being a pastor. God has asked me to serve in a different capacity, as a lay member who has dedicated his resources to Him. I never would have seen this years ago when I asked Him "Why?"*

Arpad realized again that there is no reason to worry about the future. God was answering his prayers all the time, and even when he didn't seem to get his answer right away, God was preparing one. Sitting there in the large auditorium, listening to the speaker, he felt a tugging on his heart and a yearning. There was still something he wanted, something that he had never had, a prayer he had prayed before but had yet to see fulfilled.

A Good Measure

Arpad still longed for a deeper friendship with the Lord. *How can I have a better relationship without a thirst for His Word?* he thought. *I can never seem to get past the feeling of obligation when I read the Bible. It's like a chore I do at night and then I fall asleep. It's been this way lately. I can't find the delight in it that I know I should feel, and though I don't go by my feelings, it would be so much better if I could read His Word as if there's nothing I'd rather do.*

Arpad looked at Adela, and he had a new realization. *You know, it's rather like my relationship with my wife,* he thought. *I'm so impatient and certain with how I think things should be that I often listen only for what I want to hear. And if I do listen, it is because I should as a "good" husband, instead of out of the love I have for her.*

Adela looked back at him, her eyes questioning. "Nothing," Arpad said, turning away. *I'm domineering. Sometimes I overpower her ideas, and I often don't give her much time to speak her side.* His thoughts continued to list the things he did or didn't do. *That's how I feel it is between*

A Good Measure

God and me too. But I don't know what to do about it.

The week of camp meeting zipped by. Sabbath morning on the last weekend, Jerry Page was leading out in the prayer meeting in the main auditorium, an old airplane hangar. He had organized an anointing service to take place afterward for those who had a special burden or request.

"Isn't it customary for the elders of the church to give anointing for someone who is sick or dying?" Adela asked.

"Yes," Arpad replied. "But maybe he will explain himself." He leaned forward to listen.

"The anointing service is the ultimate measure of request," Elder Page explained. "It is requesting a special measure of blessing from God. Traditionally it has been reserved only for terminally ill conditions or for those with a serious health condition. But that is not necessarily how it was designed. Anointing is not to bless the dying, but to heal the living. It is to recognize a serious physical, emotional, spiritual, mental, or social problem and meet it by putting our trust in God, even before we look to human sources; it is to turn to God first—not just at the last."

"Arpad," Adela whispered, "let's go to the anointing service, please?"

Jerry Page continued. "Anointing is not only for physical problems, but disease that sin has caused in our lives, like bad habits, hurts in our lives that continue to traumatize or cripple us, for forgiveness and for total commitment to God."

"OK," Arpad said after the meeting was over. "I think I'd like to go too."

They walked to the small auditorium where the anointing service was to take place. Elder Page made an appeal for those participating to come openly to God. "We can come to Him as we are, as long as we come." The anointing was led by a small group of pastors and those who had come to pray on behalf of the participants. Many people wanted anointing, so Arpad and Adela waited patiently. The time for the anointing service was almost over, and Arpad and Adela were last in line. When they thought they were almost out of time, they were motioned to join the group. Arpad and Adela sat down, and all the group members then introduced themselves. There were a few moments of socializing in which participants shared information about themselves. Finally Arpad explained his reason for requesting anointing.

"I would like spiritual healing," he said. "I've studied God's Word only out of duty, but now I'd like a thirst for God's Word. I want a desire that I won't be able to live from day to day without this enjoyment. I also want to have more patience when I communicate with Adela. I always seem to know the answers." The leader of the group, Tom Kapusta, nodded his head with vigor.

"I can ask the same anointing for myself," he said humbly. The group prayed for Arpad. Tom placed a dab of olive oil on his forehead in a symbol of blessing. That was all. The time was now up because the church service was about to begin.

A cool, refreshing wind blew in from the ocean on Sunday, the last day of the camp meeting, bringing with it the sounds of tents being taken down, motorhomes crunching away down the gravel camp road, and the faint scent of *Stripples*® frying. Arpad and Adela went into the large auditorium filled with metal folding chairs and pockets of mingling people. "I sure hope this meeting goes smoothly," Arpad commented. "I've been on enough committees, in enough meetings to know how frustrating and long they can be, especially when there are controversial issues at stake." During this meeting, constituents would vote whether or not to implement the Phase I fund-raising, the first effort of the Capital Campaign to raise $6 million in the next two years, and then Phase II, an effort to raise $21 million following that. The auditorium soon filled with 700 people, and Arpad and Adela, along with the other presenters, walked on stage.

"We believe in prayer, we believe in God's leading, and we've got work to do," said Jerry Page, the conference president. He continued his devotional speech by drawing several lessons from the life of Nehemiah as he led the Israelites in rebuilding Jerusalem's walls. "Much prayer, planning, cooperation of the people, and spiritual revival are the key components of success," he summarized.

"In 1995 we voted for four priorities: spiritual growth, loving fellowship and unity, mobilization of the spiritual gifts of all members, and evangelistic outreach. The Capital Campaign is a result from this vision. The ministries carried out at these conference properties and our schools are essential to the spiritual life of this conference," Elder Page continued. "Out of the goal of ministries for people arises need for facilities, buildings, camps, and funding to keep it all going. Many people don't realize why these projects are important. We're raising more than money for a campground, a summer camp, or school tuition. We're raising support to facilitate all these ministries."

Following the president's prayer, the chairmen for all three projects of the Capital Campaign then presented what was involved in their areas and why they needed support. The audience listened, an occasional cough or creak from chairs the only sounds. Then, as representatives of the volunteer fund-raising committee, it was Arpad and Adela's turn to walk to the podium to share their testimony. Arpad looked out on the sea of constituents, wondering what was happening in their collective minds. *Would they catch the vision too?* He breathed a prayer for words.

"A short time ago, if somebody had told us that we would experience God's blessing in a bigger way than ever before through fund-raising, we would have laughed. We like and welcome surprises, but this was a big one. God has a great sense of humor." He and Adela related the events that had led to their commitment.

"The challenge of the financial pledge was big, but God assured us that He would provide a way to meet it. And He did! This is a greater adventure and challenge than anything we've ever had before," Arpad said.

"The same kind of experience that we went through can be true of absolutely anybody in any situation," Adela added. "It begins with a turn-around of the heart, and for us, that happened when we gave outside of our comfort zone."

"It's not just about money," Arpad emphasized. "God can assure you with the same feeling, no matter what you return to Him. He expects in return only the gifts He has given you. For some people it is money, for some it is time, for some preaching, for some helping, for some kindness and smiles, for some knowledge, for others wisdom. God just asks you to give whatever you have."

"Committing to the Capital Campaign showed us something that we were missing in our lives," Adela said, "the blessing of being involved in God's work. The Seventh-day Adventist Church leaves personal financial decisions in the hands of each member where it belongs. We understand the biblical principle of returning tithes and offerings, but most of us never feel obligated to go beyond this. And it's true. God really doesn't need our gifts. He could accomplish His work without us, but we have been given an opportunity to work side by side with Him. This is but another chance to know Him better.

"So many people, young and old, sit in the shadow of their religion, refusing to take an active role in the ownership of their own church. 'It's the leadership's role to be involved,' we often say to ourselves. 'It's enough that I come and sit here every week, give my tithe, and, if I have small enough change, offering. And though it's definitely not all about money, what we do with our money has everything to do with the state of the heart.

"The act of giving is an investment in one's future. ' "Give, and it will be given to you," ' the promise is written. ' "A good measure, pressed down, shaken together and running over, will be poured into your lap. For with the measure you use, it

A Good Measure

will be measured to you.' '* We didn't know what measure God could pour out until we tested Him. We had to take a risk and give Him a chance. Another thing that giving did for us was to allow the Holy Spirit to ignite in our hearts a passion for God's work."

When Arpad and Adela sat down, they waited in silence, wondering what impact their words had made.

Jerry Page called for a motion to accept the Capital Campaign. "Is there a second?"

"Second." Arpad had taken out his checkbook and written out the first payment toward the pledge. He held it out to the officiator.

"All in favor?"

Arpad had never seen anything like it. Red strips of paper, indicating the vote, fluttered a crimson yes, high in the hands above almost all the constituents' heads. "All opposed?" One red flutter toward the back.

Wow! Arpad thought, *God is indeed leading in this project. Rarely is there this large a majority. This many people are ready to raise $6 million for God?* "Ushers, lock the doors, please," he called out. "We'll raise $6 million right now." The audience laughed.

"I wonder how long your high will last?" someone asked Arpad the day after he returned from the camp meeting, enthusiastic over the spiritual boost he had received from the weeklong spiritual retreat.

"I don't know," Arpad replied. "We'll see." Arpad had known this feeling before, the short-lived inspiration that fills a person for a week or so after a meaningful event, such as a week of prayer. Would it last a week? A month? Of course the strong emotions would fade somewhat, but Arpad knew that something was radically different, another something he couldn't rationalize as coincidence. He had discovered it that morning.

---
* Luke 6:38.

THE ARPAD SOO STORY

24

Stronghold

Arpad woke and stretched as he usually did, pulling away from the tight hold of sleep. Every morning he would walk outside for the newspaper, come back to the kitchen, and fix himself a strong pot of coffee to wrestle away any clinging fingers of grogginess. He would then sit down at the kitchen table with the cup of steaming comfort to read the latest scores on the sports page. Then he would say a quick prayer, read his worship text, and start his work day. His fifteen-minute study time was punctuated by calls from employees or business contacts; because early morning was the busiest time of day, he had to order the materials right away for a job site and get his employees going. This day, though, he had promised himself to start his routine differently. "I'm going to dedicate to God my best time," he said.

He poured himself some Starbucks® coffee, added cream and sugar, and opened his Bible. Twenty minutes later he was still studying Romans, fascinated by what he was reading. "Lord," he prayed, "please let these words stay with me all day." The phone didn't ring until he had finished devouring the chapter. *Did I read my Bible this whole time?* he asked himself. *I actually enjoyed it.* Remembering his prayer, he shook his head in amazement. *Wow! I wonder how long this will last?*

Throughout the next few weeks, he experienced the same phenomenon. He read for fifteen or twenty minutes in the morning, the phone silent the whole time. He found himself looking forward to this time, and he started waking a little earlier. The Bible continued to pull him in, and he began underlining promises that inspired him. Only after he had established his new habit did the phone begin ringing as usual. Arpad valued his new experience with Scripture so much that he did not answer the phone when it rang. He couldn't start his day without his nourishment from God.

Every day when he left for the construction site the words didn't stay with just him; he was sharing them with others. Many times he found himself in circumstances on the job site with the verses he had read that morning coming clearly into focus, providing exactly what he needed in that situation. Sometimes the reading guided his own actions or speech, and sometimes he shared it with an employee. *I forgot that reading Holy Scripture could be this practical*, he thought. *I was trying to be a better Christian by reading more of the Bible, but, again, my priorities were wrong. My business and my involvement in so many things came first, and they crowded out His words.* God had changed that. Arpad was just as involved and busy as before, but reading his Bible had now become the highlight of his day.

During the second week in October, several months after the camp meeting, Arpad and his three friends in the For Heaven's Sake quartet were invited to perform for the annual Central California Conference Men's Retreat at Wawona, the summer camp in Yosemite National Park. On Friday night,

IN HIS HANDS

the speaker talked to the men's group about the ways evil comes into our lives and stakes out little footholds. Over time, these footholds turn into strongholds.

The speaker prompted the men to form small groups in the cafeteria. Their job was to recognize problem strongholds in their lives, to share with each other, and to pray for each other. "The purpose is to acknowledge those areas in your life where you have lost control, to name them, and to gain the courage to face them." It was chilly in the mountains, and the men gathered in the cafeteria around the burning fire in the big rock fireplace. Arpad, with his friends Brian and Warren, was placed in a small group with Brad, a man who had arrived late at the retreat.

Arpad, Brian, and Warren shared their strongholds. Brad's turn came.

"You know," he said, "where I feel that I am out of control is in my need and love for coffee."

Arpad stared at him. "Coffee?"

"Yes," Brad continued. "I work as a computer programmer, and I can never live without it, whether at work all day or at home. I can't break this addiction."

Arpad looked at Warren and almost smiled, trying to keep his jaw from dropping.

Here we are talking about our deepest, darkest temptations, and this guy talks about coffee? Get real! What's wrong with coffee? Arpad could practically smell the rich aroma as the morning sun washed the windows. He thought about the For Heaven's Sake practices. Their rule was that the person to show up late bought everyone their favorite coffee at Starbucks. *I love coffee,* Arpad thought. *The taste, the company, the ritual. I'd sure be in trouble without it. How can something so useful and delicious be an evil thing?*

Then it was time to split up into twos to pray for each other. Arpad's partner was Brad. *Ha! Just my luck,* Arpad thought. But as he was praying, his attitude changed. *I know how he feels,* Arpad thought. *If I don't make it to the coffee pot, by two in the afternoon my head starts hammering. I've tried to quit before, but I can't stand the withdrawal pains. Coffee controls my life too.* He prayed sincerely for Brad, empathizing with his struggle.

Saturday morning, Arpad got out of bed. There was no coffee at the camp, and though Arpad had brought his own, he didn't have a desire to make it. He didn't have a headache, and he didn't feel the heavy stupor that he usually felt when he missed his coffee break. He went through the whole day without coffee. Sunday was the same—no withdrawal symptoms. He returned home. The desire for coffee was gone. He read his Bible without it in the mornings. He bought hot chocolate at Starbucks instead of coffee. "I can't explain it," Arpad told Warren. "I prayed for Brad, and God completely healed *me*. I have never even had a headache."

Arpad's view of God kept growing larger. He read the Bible verse in Malachi 3:10, which spoke of returning out of one's income to the Lord. " 'Test me in this,' says the Lord Almighty, 'and see if I will not throw open the floodgates of heaven and pour out so much blessing that you will not have room enough for it.' " *Not enough room to receive?* Arpad thought. *With God it keeps getting better. I think this promise goes beyond giving tithe to giving one's all.* A passage from an Adventist author written in the early 1900s caught his eye. In the story about Jesus' life, Jesus had just turned the water at the wedding feast into wine. It seemed as though it had been written for him.

> As men set forth the best wine first, then afterward that which is worse, so does the world with its gifts.... But the gifts of Jesus are ever fresh and new. The feast that He provides for the soul never fails to give satisfaction and joy. Each new gift increases the capacity

of the receiver to appreciate and enjoy the blessings of the Lord. He gives grace for grace. There can be no failure of supply. If you abide in Him, the fact that you receive a rich gift today insures the reception of a richer gift tomorrow.... With every fresh revelation of His love, He declares to the receptive heart, "Believest thou? thou shalt see greater things than these." John 1:50 (*The Desire of Ages,* p. 148).

As a volunteer fund raiser, he was about to see what God could do in others' lives when they gave Him the opportunity. As for himself, he smiled knowing the best was still to come.

The Bold Question

Being a fund raiser and financial supporter wasn't exactly what Arpad had envisioned as his life's ministry. Because he had grown up with the Communists telling him everything he couldn't do, he had developed a love of risk-taking for God's cause. He had enjoyed working with underground smuggling in Romania, but now he was asked to do the opposite: boldly ask people for their financial support.

"I had almost lost the vision of risking for God," Arpad told Adela. "I've prayed that I could somehow return to God's ministry, but I hadn't foreseen this. I realize that I have opportunities to serve God now that I never could have achieved as a minister."

Soon after the constituency meeting, the volunteer fundraising committee met to plan how they were going to raise the $6 million for the Capital Campaign. The fund raisers' job would be to provide information about the project to people who were looking for worthy causes to support. Awareness dinners would provide potential donors with this information and answer their questions. A few weeks later, so that the guests had had time to consider making a gift, Arpad and Adela, along with the other volunteers, would make appointments to meet with each of them.

"How are we going to know how much money to ask people to pledge?" Warren Hamrick asked. "Shouldn't we just let people come to their own conclusion about what they want to give?"

"Of course," Adela said. "Remember, Arpad, how much we thought we'd give when Brook Sadler first asked us? Only several thousand. But if we had pledged that, nothing much would have changed within us because it wasn't a difficult pledge. Then Marie asked us to give so much more than we ever dreamed of. We would never have considered giving the amount she asked because we were still too invested in ourselves. It was the challenge that opened our eyes."

"But who are we to judge how much money to ask for?" Warren said.

"It's human nature to be protective of one's material assets," Arpad reflected. "There's a part of me that feels guilty asking for money, even though it's for a good cause."

"I know," Adela said. "I feel the same way. Now I empathize with Marie when she was so bold with us. It's not easy to be so daring. But remember, many people want to give, and neglecting to ask people for donations to a project that will benefit so many people would be denying others the privilege of giving. We underestimate the blessing that comes through giving."

"Wasn't it Jesus who said that 'it is more blessed to give than to receive'?" Arpad asked. "It surely has proven true in my life. I read a quotation yesterday, what was it? 'It is no longer our resources that limit our decisions; it is our decisions that limit our resources.'* That's so true with God. But what about the amount to request?"

---

* U. Thant.

The Bold Question

"What a sticky question," Kathy said. "The conference has asked us to plan our requests ahead of time. How are we going to do this?"

"Well," said Arpad, scratching his chin. "I read an interesting passage in my Bible this morning. A man goes to a neighbor at midnight and asks him for bread because a friend has come to visit. 'I don't have anything to give you,' the man tells his neighbor. The neighbor answers from inside the house. 'Don't bother me. The door is now shut, and my children and I are in bed. I cannot rise and give to you.' Then Jesus said that even though the neighbor would not rise and give to the man because he was his friend, yet because of his persistence he would rise and give him as much as he needs.[2] It's because he asks boldly. Here's what I think. Let's look at this list of names and then beside each one, write down how much we would ask them. After that, let's average the figures and use that as what we ask."

The rest agreed. Arpad took to heart the Bible passage he had read that morning and wrote bold figures. They would later learn that the amount they had chosen for each name usually worked well.

Arpad and Adela traveled all over Central California getting to know the donors personally. Arpad loved meeting people and sharing his experiences. This kind of work was challenging. Arpad and Adela had to find the right time, the right setting, the right questions, and the right way to promote the campaign. But through meetings with potential donors, Arpad and Adela grew closer to people and were surprised often. Some people who they didn't think could afford much, gave more than what was expected. Arpad and Adela saw sides of people they would never have imagined.

---

[2] Luke 11:5-8.

IN HIS HANDS

"Strange, isn't it," Adela said, "how we ask people for an enormous amount of money and suddenly we're the best of friends with them!"

"I know," Arpad said. "We can never judge people. As the Bible says, ' "Man looks at the outward appearance, but the Lord looks at the heart." '* We've seen certain sides of people we couldn't believe or imagine, but we're starting to understand that God knows their hearts and that it is so important to accept people as they are. We've become close friends with people we never thought we could relate to."

Of course, not everybody could commit; some had limiting circumstances and some were not interested. Many donated a lesser amount. Some were already involved with other projects. The disappointments of being turned down didn't hurt Arpad and Adela as much as they had thought it would.

Arpad, Adela, and their fund-raising partners, Warren and Kathy, sat together in the Soo living room one late afternoon. A light breeze blew through the open window, the cooling effect of the Pacific Ocean several miles away.

"I've learned to trust God in this," Adela said after one rejection. "This is His project, and I can't take the rebuff personally."

"It's a lot of effort to volunteer time to God's work, but God blesses this time we're giving Him. I love getting to know people one on one," Arpad said. "And working so closely with the Church, and seeing the organization working, it's easy to criticize leaders, but working with the Capital Campaign has rebuilt my trust in the Church leadership."

"There are so many good things that happen when we give to God," Adela said, her heart full. "Just seeing what has happened in the lives of our friends has inspired me so much. For many people time is much harder to give than money."

---

*1 Samuel 16:7.

The Bold Question

"I agree," Warren said, "but time is no less fulfilling." Warren, an architect, had also been asked to be a part of the planning and implementation team for the expansion of Camp Wawona. "I was glad to be a part of the decision making with the vision of how renovating Camp Wawona can best represent God," he reflected. "It struck me, too, that building projects are frequently mentioned in Scripture, and when God, the Master Architect, gave instruction, He always had the best quality in mind."

"Yeah," piped up Kathy, his wife. "Not once did He ask for the cheapest or more inferior materials or design. When giving the plans to Moses for the tabernacle, God didn't say 'Use whatever materials you have lying around.' He didn't just say, 'Use some linens and some gold.' No. His instructions were to use the 'best' linens and the 'finest' gold."

Warren smiled. "And I think that's what He expects of us today, the finest materials, the finest design, and the finest time that we can give Him."

"It's the same with building our houses," Arpad added. "Should we expect less for God?"

"I can't say enough about the spiritual enrichment I felt as I donated many hours and many dollars to a cause I feel is being led by our Creator," Warren said, looking at his wife. "It's as if I have been crafted into a tool through my experience and my education."

"A tool that has been sharpened," added his wife, "and now is finally put into service in just the right way, at the right time."

"You both can relate to this," Warren said to Arpad and Adela. "The rewards have spilled into my professional practice so that I can multiply my service in many other areas. I never would have guessed that God would work this way." He shook his head.

"You know," said Kathy. "I believe that God expects us to return our talents, and if we stand up and begin with a single step, we will soon be running and leaping and praising His name." The other three nodded.

"That reminds me of our friends, the DeVries," said Adela. "The DeVries took the challenge, raised by the Central California Conference stewardship department, and started giving double tithe. As they followed this practice, Don, a research chemist, kept rising in the managerial circle for Shell, to the laboratory manager position. Their lives prospered financially. As they got involved with the Capital Campaign project, the DeVries' lives prospered spiritually. Before they had been distant, but now they are deeply involved with the Church and school as well. As they increased their giving, the Lord kept blessing them. They learned that there is no way to out-give the Lord."

Arpad, sitting next to Adela, grinned, his voice fervent. "I can believe it because of my own experience."

"That's the only way we ever can," Adela said. "The only way we can."

THE ARPAD SOO STORY
26

Another Gate

"There's a land that is fairer than day." The strains of the old hymn floated through the church. "And by faith we can see it afar." Arpad lifted his voice in harmony with the quartet, looking above the listeners' heads to the ceiling high above. "For the Father looks over the way." The notes rose and fell. "To prepare us a dwelling place there." As the bass, baritone, and tenors blended in a cappella voice, Arpad's mind slipped momentarily back in time.

In Romania, Arpad had seen the Western world as a gate to heaven. He had studied the lives of the pioneers of the Seventh-day Adventist Church. He had longed to be a part of its mission. Locked in Communism, Arpad had dreamed of living his beliefs in a free land. But he had longed for more than religious freedom.

From the information that could penetrate to him from America, everything there seemed to be of super-high quality. The people were beautiful, tall, happy, well-dressed, and clean. The cars were gorgeous, the technology amazing. When he suddenly was able to go to America, he felt fulfilled. "This is it," he remembered saying, looking around at the cleanness of the country, the organization of the American society: the economic system, the courts, the hospitals, the Christian schools, and the church. He heard the beautiful organ music from the huge church in Loma Linda and saw the manicured arboretum of Loma Linda University. The beauty and wealth and abundance overwhelmed him. Things were really as he had dreamed, from the smallest to the largest things.

It wasn't long before he realized he was far from heaven. The more TV and movies he watched, the more newspapers and books he read, he saw the struggles of the "perfect" society: fights over drugs, killings, degrading entertainment, racism. It deflated him.

I put my hopes in earthly things, Arpad thought. *My citizenship here is temporary. Someday I will be a citizen of His heavenly kingdom, this citizenship given to me not on my own merits or works, but based on what God has done for me.* In his memory, he saw the Czechoslovakian gate lifting to let him into Austria and freedom, but now a picture of another gate blazed in his mind, and it was swinging wide in some not-too-distant future to let him in. There, another welcome sign awaited him, where he would weep for joy.

"In the sweet by and by we shall meet on that beautiful shore," the chorus rang. When the song ended, it would be Arpad's turn to share his story with the listeners. Arpad's thoughts rose beyond the ceiling in a silent prayer. "Lord, if my story can make one person open up and listen to You, then the suffering I went through will have been worth it all." What would he say, he didn't have time to think, but he knew what was bubbling up from his being. The words were in his soul.

"There's nothing to worry about except we forget how God has led us in the past,"* Arpad would say. "God allowed me to learn from my mistakes, even though I didn't deserve any-

---

*See Ellen G. White, *Life Sketches*, 196.

Another Gate

thing. I would like to see anyone give me one reason how such things could happen in my life outside of God. I am His miracle. I'm far from perfect, but God's presence is so powerful in my life that I see a constant light, a constant beacon in my thoughts and business decisions every day. The same experience can be true of anyone in any situation. It begins with a turn-around of the heart. I always wondered what God's plan was for my life, and now I know. I still am called to work for God, but I know that I don't have to be a minister to do this. He calls me to be a risk-taker for Him in everything, to trust Him with my finances, my time, my family, and my life. I wouldn't have known the measure that God could pour out upon me until I gave Him the chance."

Arpad sang the last stanza. "To our bountiful Father above, we will offer a tribute of praise, for the glorious gift of His love, and the blessings that hallow our days. In the sweet by and by we shall meet on the beautiful shore. In the sweet by and by we shall meet on that beautiful shore." As the harmony faded, he turned to the audience. The words that flowed from his heart were filled with praise.

If you enjoyed this book, you'll enjoy these as well:

Mission Pilot
Eileen Lantry. The true adventures of David Gates, a missionary pilot who repeatedly experienced the miracles of God in his life. Through hijackings, prison, and many other narrow escapes, David proves that living for God is still the highest adventure.
0-8163-1870-0. Paperback.
US$12.99, Can$20.49.

Chosen
Ron and Nancy Rockey. The true story of Ron Rockey's journey from prison literal and spiritual freedom proves that God is behind and at work in all the storms in our lives to bring about a good end. Includes a personal study guide/self-help section.
0-8163-1900-6. Paperback.
US$12.99, Can$20.49.

Beyond the Veil of Darkness
Esmie Branner. A heart-pounding account of the struggles, hardships, and courageous triumph of a young Christian woman who refused to deny her faith in Christ despite the physical and mental abuse of a Muslim husband.
0-8163-1713-5. Paperback.
US$9.99, Can$15.49.

Order from your ABC by calling 1-800-765-6955, or get online and shop our virtual store at www.adventistbookcenter.com.
- Read a chapter from your favorite book
- Order online
- Sign up for email notices on new products

Prices subject to change without notice.